I0659256

NO APOLOGIES

The final book of the series Double Back

By: Author Jamie

NO APOLOGIES

This book is the fictional work of the author. All opinions and expressions are solely those of the author. The characters are fictional and do not depict, portray or represent any particular person(s)

ISBN: 978-0-9966466-5-9

Edited by N. Miller

Cover Design by Outsourcing Unlimited LLC

Printed in the United States of America

NO APOLOGIES

Dedication page

I dedicate this book to my hot and spicy 5 piece!

NO APOLOGIES

Acknowledgments

I want to start off by thanking the CREATOR for giving me such great gifts and the knowledge on how to use them.

I also want to thank friends and family who have been on this journey with me from the beginning.

I want to give a special thanks to Black Lyfe Publications, for letting all my words have a place to call home. Thank you for supporting my dreams and helping to make them bigger. Black Lyfe 4 Lyfe! Xoxoxo

To all of my supporters new and old thank you because it's you who really make any of this possible!

NO APOLOGIES

GOLDIE 1

Wow! She is so fucking gorgeous, just looking at her make a nigga wanna buss a nut. Looking at them pretty ass titties, peeking from up under the cover. How did a nigga like me get so fucking lucky? With all the shit I have been through with her, and without her, I can't believe that she is still here riding with me. She did say she was gonna be here for me no matter what, and I guess she never lied about that. I could stare at her all damn day long. Fuck! My dick getting hard as hell right now. Little does she know, she about to get dicked down at two in the fucking morning.

Any other time, I would be out wondering what pussy I can get deep into without all the trouble of bitches falling in love and what not. Sometimes it did go that way; all they wanted was this monster of a dick game, and then others wanted the man, and the dick damn shame too. I have come across some fine, sexy ass women in my life, and the only person that held it for real was Jas. I was telling them women all kind of shit like; have my baby, you got the best pussy I have ever had, no I don't have a women and all. Because I knew the wanted me, I could get away with the shit.

I can't believe I am sitting here thinking about other pussy, when the only one that truly matters is laying right next to me. Shit! If I could have had a threesome with Jas, and Indigo that shit would have been epic. Damn! I am going to hell for sure.

Laying here with my woman, and thinking about threesome and shit. Well its official, I got major problems. I just wish niggas could fuck, get a nut, and come on home to their woman without any issues, of course that is not the fucking real world; at least not the world I live in. I would surly move if I ever found a place of existence like that.

Look at her moving all sultry in her sleep look, like she doing a slow whine with every twist. The covers slid further off of her breast, nipples looking like milk duds; they are so damn big. Looking at what I got here, if I ever found out some shit about her in these fucking streets fucking these niggas, other than that lame ass nigga she tried to have fuck the taste of me out of her mouth; that's the one and only nigga I didn't go too hard on her about. Because I knew what she was trying to do.

Let me grab this Hennessy off the night stand, and take another shot. My mind is all over the damn place right now, and it's about damn time she get some of daddy's dick. After gulping my damn shot of Hennessy, I slid over to her, slid the covers completely off of her already naked body, did a slight rub to my dick; that motherfucker hard as penitentiary steel. Leaning over her face planting soft kisses over her face calling her name with ever kiss. "Yes bae."

NO APOLOGIES

"You look so fucking good. I just want to eat the fuck out of your pussy; have you reaching for oxygen and shit." Still kissing her tracing her mouth with my tongue; kissing her neck, shoulders, lawd the titties. These nipples are hard as diamonds. Circling her harden left nipple in my mouth, sucking and grazing my teeth across her nipples. "Mmmmmm...Goldie," she moaned. "Yes baby. You like that shit don't you?" "Mmmm Hmmmm."

Switching to the right nipple circling, sucking and kissing is making it harder than it was before I started. Pushing her legs open further with my knees, as my mouth rest on her perfect mounds, letting my tongue tease her nipples, while my hands are caressing her breast. Pushing both breast together, so I can satisfy both nipples. "Shit! Jas baby, you got the perfect ass nipples in the world," she said. "Bite these nipples baby that shit making my pussy wet as fuck."

I stopped to look at her and a smile came across my face. Knowing what I was about to do to her was driving me insane. Jas voice was barely above a whisper when she spoke. "Why you stop baby?" she asked. "I am just admiring all this beauty I have in front of me, feeling your heat from Paradise on my legs, looking at your breast that has nipples standing at attention for me."

NO APOLOGIES

Back to me putting passion marks on her breast; slowly easing my tongue down the center of her breast, licking under them. Licking her stomach, her navel, and inhaling the aromatic scent from her paradise got me ready to erupt like a fucking volcano. Damn! She has the prettiest shaved pussy I have ever seen. Her lips look like butterfly wings on her clit. She looks like she is about to cum her damn self. Pussy wet as fuck right now. Let me handle this business, so she can go back to sleep.

Kissing the outside of her pussy then the inside; tracing the outside of her lips with my tongue, opening up her pussy, so I can suck generously on her engorged clit. I hear deep moaning from her, as

NO APOLOGIES

I flick my tongue slow then build up speed giving her the three finger stroke; telling her to cum now. "Ooooh baby...Goldie that's it baby. Fuck! you gonna make me cum too soon." I smiled, well that is the point. Knowing she was almost near. I remove my fingers, and dart my tongue in and out of her pussy, and thumbed her clit with added pressure. With my left hand I insert a glaze coated finger in her ass. Watching my baby roll her hips, and push her pussy deeper into my mouth, felt so fucking good. Damn she tasted like a honey coated peach, fuck!

"Damn it Goldie! Fuck baby it's here. Oooooooh fuck! Its hereee!" she passionately screamed.

NO APOLOGIES

"That's it Jas give me that damn nut all of it!" Feeling her cream ooze out of her, and into my mouth, is the best fucking thing ever. I place my hands under her ass, and help elevate her some; as she continues to erupt in my mouth. Her body is shaking, I look up and see her reaching for shit that ain't even there. What a wonderful sight to see. I take one more long pull on her clit, and suck out the rest of her juices before I give her the signal with a light tap on her thigh to turn over.

I hop off the bed, stand at the foot of the bed, and watch her move backwards towards me. I pointed my dick towards her ass, that way she would feel how close she was. Her left ass cheek hit the tip of my dick. Sliding my dick from her pussy to her ass, hell! I want everything wet as fuck. Sliding in her tight pussy; feeling her grip my dick as soon as I get in. Lifting her around her waist, I bend my legs slightly while she locked her feet around me. Her head is completely down on the bed, ass on my stomach, and me pounding away. Fuck! She screaming like I am killing her. She gonna remember this damn dick the next time she try to have someone fuck the taste of me out of her mouth. "Take this dick baby take all this shit."

"I'm taking it Goldie. That's it fuck me hard and deep." Damn! I should have had my Timberlands on for grip, but that's okay, I got her ass right where

NO APOLOGIES

I want her. Head down- ass up. Locking in my arms around her waist, and lifting her up, so she can't run from the dick. Pounding round for round, mile for mile. Looking down at my dick, as it slides out damn! My shit is wet as fuck. I am gonna knock the bottom out of this pussy. "Oh shit! Golide!" She screamed. "Yea babe, this dick all for you damn it!"

"Don't stop, don't stopppp!" she begged. "Stop for what?" Watching her ass bounce every time I hit. "Lock your legs around me baby." Stroke, pound, stroke, pound, deep stroking her; I know she is about to give in. "Throw that pussy back Jas," I said. "Fuck Goldie, baby I am about to cum again," She yelled. **"FUCK...JAS!"**

NO APOLOGIES

"That's it baby cum for daddy fuck cum for me."
Man I am trying to touch her fucking brain. She
don't even know, all the shit I got running through
my fucking head should be against the fucking law.
I am here fucking her like she the last pussy on
earth, but damn! Why is my fucking brain on mo'
pussy like really. What the hell is wrong with my
ass? "That's it baby keep throwing that ass at me,
grip this dick fuck Jas I am about to paint your
walls...fuck baby!"

"Goldie oh shit! This shit is mind blowing baby.
Don't nut in me. No Goldie!" I am about to let this
load go fuck shit let me ease her on the bed so I can
let loose. "Jas, its coming baby fuck

it's....**CUMINGGGGGGGGGGG**!" Shit let me slide out this pussy and jag this motherfucker on her ass, before I fuck around and get her pregnant again, we don't need another abortion around this motherfucker. Damn look at my baby ass covered with all my damn thick cream. If this shit ain't a perfect sight I don't know what is.

"That's it babe rub that ass on this dick." She just don't know how bad I want to slide the head back up in her tight ass pussy. What the fuck? Kissing her softly on her back, watching her ease down onto the bed in a lying position on the bed yeah she done. "Mmmmmm fuck Goldie that shit was so fucking good. Damn! Baby you have given me my damn knock out drops," She said. "Well, I aim to please baby. Anytime I am in this pussy, I am always gonna give you your knock out drops."

"Can you run my shower baby?" She asked. "No problem I got you Jas," Lightly tapping her on the ass; she does a cute little wiggle for me, heading down the hall to the bathroom, and pulling the shower doors back; full steam shower. I know her ass is probably sleep by now. Let me hop in here first. Stepping out the shower, and grabbing the plush blue towel off the back of the door; that's hanging next to Jas red plush towel. Looking in the full length mirror, as I wrap the towel around my waist; looking at one fine specimen of a man.

NO APOLOGIES

Muscular build, six pack, dreads flowing like a river and god has blessed me to be very well endowed. Shiiiiddddd no wonder this women gone crazy. Just saying all that shit to myself I couldn't do shit but laugh.

I began walking back in the room, and tapping Jas on the ass to wake her up; so she can take her shower, and wash the now dried up cum off her ass. "Jas baby get up the shower is waiting on you."

"Okay baby." Jas lazily peeled herself off the bed and stumbled into the bathroom. I made the bed up, oiled up my body, and climbed back into bed with a hard ass dick in my hand. This shit is fucking ridiculous. I just finished fucking the life out of my woman, and my dick hard again. Stroking this motherfucker is not making it no better. Little do Jas know, when she get back in here, she gonna have to put that head game to work. Hell, I don't call her head hunter for nothing.

NO APOLOGIES

JASMINE 2

I can't believe this shit is happening. I got my man back, I am back in the home where we are going to raise Rasheeda, and many more babies in. I knew it was only going to be a matter of time that he get his shit together. I don't see how much longer he thought I was going to put up with his shit. I mean granted I love him, but damn, my love does have a limit. Most of the time, I try my hardest to be the woman I know he wants, and needs. Hell! I am not going to let him drive me crazy as fuck with him sleeping with this woman, and that woman.

Pussy will have a man fucked up. He will forget about his woman, his relationship, and anything that makes sense when it comes to that powerful word **PUSSY!** I was always told by my Aunt Fatty, that all men are intrigued by some new pussy but they won't hesitate to fuck some old pussy either. She use to say "Pussy talks chile, and don't you ever forget it." Aunt Fatty always made sure that I knew the ends, and outs of men, and pussy. I use to get extremely mad when Goldie would step out, but when Aunt Fatty gave me a refreshers course on the power that we as women hold, I started to understand that lust is stronger than love. She would let me know that as a woman if your man is fucking up maybe your pussy ain't talking loud enough, I didn't quite understand what she meant by that but I soon found out.

NO APOLOGIES

Look at him laying here, just as peaceful as he want. I guess being a headhunter will knock any man to sleep. Glancing at the illuminated clock on the night stand, fuck! its damn near five in the morning. His ass better be glad it's the weekend, so that means him in the streets; me with my girls, and baby girl with her mom. Goldie really has been trying to stay on the straight and narrow, since he knew that I was seeing Derwin. Man that mother fucker was so damn fine...shit! Just the thought of him is making my pussy wet right now. The sad part is, I know if I called him right now, he would be game to fuck me senseless and lick me dry. Poor thang; he was so smitten with me that just the pure excitement he brought to was nothing short of awesome.

Like a typical man, he started fucking around with Chanta' skank ass. I am not saying she a skank for fucking him, hell! she is doing what comes natural. I am saying she a skank for having any dealings with him after he and I broke up. But through it all, if my heart was not right here with Goldie, I would have been with Derwin no questions asked. I wonder do Chanta' know he got with her to spite me? Maybe not. Hell! She really thought Goldie wanted her ass. I am sure he wanted to fuck, but have a relationship with her? Hell no!

NO APOLOGIES

This motherfucker sleep, and I am wide awake now, pussy throbbing and shit. I need another fix but after fucking, and getting his dick sucked; he down for the count. Hell! I want to watch television, but he hates the light. I guess I will take my ass to the guest bedroom, and watch television in there. Let me grab my red satin robe and slippers, and get out of here before I find a limp dick in my mouth. Did I just hear my phone buzz? Hell no! I must be hearing shit. If it did buzz, it means it's a damn text which can't be too damn important at five in the morning, and whoever it is didn't call. No time for fuckery this time of the morning; it's still dark out too.

NO APOLOGIES

Damn! When the last time someone cleaned up in here? The covers are all over the bed, and the DVD player is still going. The television is turned off. Must have been one of those late nights we had an argument, and I made his ass sleep in here. Well, let me just close the door, cut the television on, and see what Goldie was watching in here; as if I don't already know. I press play, and just as I thought, a porn. Big asses and big titties, is the first thing I see. Well I guess this is what I will be watching till I fall asleep. Climbing up in this king size comfortable ass bed, and looking at this shit on this T.V. is making me hornier than a motherfucker. Pussy nice and smooth, fat ass clit, and nipples hard as diamonds.

NO APOLOGIES

Hell! looks like I could have done the same shit this women doing only better. Caressing my breast, rolling my nipples through my fingers, Mmmmmm- this shit is feeling so damn good. Pussy leaking so damn bad, I need to fuck and be fucked now. Reaching over in the nightstand drawer, way in the back, I found my 10' Bill. Nice, thick and ready to have my pussy juices all over this plastic dick. Mmmmmm rubbing the clit with the head of Bill, looking down at my swollen clit...shit feel like I want to bust right now.

My pussy acting like it wants to grab the head, and suck him in all ready. Damn! the head of Bill is glistening all damn ready. Sliding the head in ever so smoothly, damn! hope I don't moan too damn loud. Sliding Bill in and out of me with ease; gripping him every time he slides in…. fuck! This shit feels so damn good. I should have came in here a long time ago. Mmmmmm…Bill…fuck me baby! Yes, like that. Don't stop! I am so damn close to cumming; squeezing my left and right nipples as Bill moves in, and out of me fuck baby…**FUUUUCCCKKKK!!!!!!!**

Rolling my orgasm out through my hips, and through my pussy; fucking Bill until I am completely relieved of my sweet creamy nut. *Panting* Oh fuck! This is what I needed, I hope Goldie didn't hear me. Jumping as I heard a knock on the door.

NO APOLOGIES

"Goldie?" I asked. "Yeah baby it's me I was trying to wait until you and Bill was finished." Goldie and I fell the fuck out laughing. "So now that you and Bill are finished, let me show you what some real dick for that ass," he responded. "Goldie go on, I just wore this pussy out, and here you come trying to make sure you wear it out some more." Yeah hearing her get off on that fake ass Bill is always cool with me, as long as it ain't no real ass nigga that I would have to fuck up for diving in my damn pussy.

Standing at the edge of the bed watching her, watching me as I stand here naked as a motherfucker; Look at that fat ass clit talking to me. I knew she was going to open them damn legs and let me see all that cum she just released. "Damn Jas that pussy fat as hell nipples hard as fuck, yeah baby it's time to fuck!" And I wasn't playing. "You ain't said shit but a damn word baby come get this pussy." Yes lawd I am about to touch all of her insides, as fucking horny as I am right now damn! Looking up at the clock on the wall shit Rasheeda will be getting up in about an hour to watch those damn cartoons. No time for sensual foreplay straight fucking.

Climbing on top of her, dick hard as fuck. I could drive a hole straight through the bed, kissing her soft ass lips, squeezing her nipples, hearing her moan is like a fucking aphrodisiac. These big ass nipples; swirling around on my tongue. "Slide that dick in daddy. Shit I need this." I couldn't help but say "You ready baby? You know I am about to give you what you want." Aww, shit is like sliding into heaven. Shit! "Yes baby lock them legs behind me." Stroking deep.

With every stroke I hear either...oh shit or uhhhhh, damn she is sounding sexy.

Placing her legs on my shoulders so I can lean into her, you better believe her knees are touching her damn ears. Quick pumps, then slide out and slide right back in; deep long strokes. "Yes baby that's it pop that pussy back Jas." She did as she was told I never have to worry about her denying me. "Fuck me harder, shit Goldie your dick game is serious baby."

"That's cause you fucking with a 9 ½ to death." Fuck! This pussy is on point. Damn, the pussy be talking to me like a motherfucker. Shit! I need to pocket this mother fucker wherever I go. I am addicted to the pussy. "Jas. Fuck! The way you throwing the pussy baby, shit a nigga ready to bust." I said. "No baby, hold that shit.'

Letting her legs down off my shoulders, I spread them eagle, and press down on her inner thighs, to do push-ups in her shit. Damn! She shutting her pussy as tight as fuck, and no sound is coming out.

NO APOLOGIES

Yes lawd, I told her I was ready to bust. "You like this shit baby...fuck is this what you want?"

"Hell yes Goldie! Fuck baby...Ooooh fuck, hold on wait, wait." Did she just put her hand on my chest, in a fucked up attempt to stop me or slow me down? She has just fucked up, she know I hate that shit with a fucking passion! Keeping my hands on her inner thighs; while on my knees, sliding in and out of her, faster and faster. Pound for pound, round for round. I hear my name ring out like bullets. Balls slapping on her ass, she can't move; I have her lower body pinned down. "Goldieee! Goldieee! Goldieee..... I am cumminnnnnn....babeeeeeeeee!"

NO APOLOGIES

Driving in harder, faster, I see her cream covering my dick fuck I am about to paint the outside of her fucking pussy or her mouth, it don't fucking matter. Grunting with every thrust I give her, letting her know I am super close. **"Ahhh....SHIT! UGHHHHHHHH! FUUCCKK!"** Sliding out and jagging this motherfucker on her clit; watching our juices mesh together. Fuck! This shit coming from my damn toes. I knew I was gonna come hard as fuck. Damn! She rubbing this shit all in her pussy. This some sexy looking shit. Hell she sexy as fuck.

Panting.

Letting the last few drops leak out of me before I hear the pitter patter of little feet. "Damn Goldie what has gotten into you?" Slapping the head of my dick on her clit trying to see where this conversation is going. "What you mean ma?"

"I am just saying you are like pumped up on sex juice or something. Granted, we have amazing sex all the fucking time, but last night and this morning, you were fucking me like you just came home from the pen doing a five year bit."

"Jas you just got some bomb ass pussy baby, and I just feel like I can't never get enough of you. Which makes me feel like, I have to give you one hundred percent of me." I can't believe that's the line he came up with. I guess knowing your woman was fucking someone else, will make any man perform to his best ability. But as of lately, Goldie ass has been going all out on this pussy.

Putting me in different positions, and shit, just being extremely extra with the sex. Now don't get me wrong, I am not complaining one bit. I know his ass trying to secure this pussy. It ain't got shit to do with me having no bomb ass pussy. I have always had bomb ass sex, and he still wasn't all extra like this. Guess it's true, if your pussy talking loud enough you will get his attention.

Well, now that we have

gotten that beautiful

shit out of the way.

Let's fast forward a

month from now and

see who the fuck we run

into.

NO APOLOGIES

Derwin & Chanta' 3

"Derwin!" Is this crazy ass chick yelling my name like she the damn police and shit? What the fuck is wrong with her ass? I knew I should have left her ass alone, but ol' no. The night Jasmine let me go, I decided to go to Mr. Browns for a few drinks, and guess who the fuck I run into...her ass. Yes, we had drinks and talked, and I let her grind that fat ass all up against my dick on the dance floor.

Stumbling out of the damn place at two in the morning had both of us headed back to my place and of course, I banged her until I couldn't bang no more. Yeah, all the frustration I was feeling after leaving Jasmine house, I took it out on her pussy that night. She must have been feeling some sort of way about her damn self because she tried to out fuck me. It's like we were in a race to see who can fuck the hardest, and the fastest. "Derwin!"

God will somebody take me out of my fucking misery with this chick. I can't even sit in my own damn man cave and get my thoughts together, without her screaming my fucking name. It's like her ass is bipolar or something. Looking down at my dick, telling him that he has done it once again; turned a chick stark crazy over the sex game.

"What the hell do you want Chanta'? I am trying to relax for a moment!" Fuck! I hear her ass marching across the living room floor. Oh no, fuck here she come. I really don't have time for this shit not right. Now it's my weekend off from the dealership. Even though I own it, I still have to go in from time to time to make sure things are still running smoothly.

"Derwin what the hell you mean what do I want? I want you to come up stairs and get out of this damn basement, come keep me company," She said. "Chanta', this is not just a basement, it's a man cave, where I come to relax watch sports on sixty inches, and play games at my leisure. I mean what the fuck Chanta', by the way, weren't you on your way home anyway?" As she stood her ass on the steps, probably just as naked as she was when

NO APOLOGIES

I left her laying in her own juices, I continued to watch ESPN. I was not about to engage in a crazy conversation with her. Nope not right now I got other shit on my mind.

"Fuck you Derwin! I get sick of your ass getting in these fucked up ass moods of yours, and taking the shit out on me. Like I don't have no damn feelings. Fuck you! Fuck you! Fuck you!" Now, the right thing to do was to go run after her after I heard her stomp back up the downstairs. But all I could do was nod my damn head. She was right. I fuck her, and keep her around so I don't have to think of Jasmine. After all the shit is over, I come down here and try and figure out a way to get her back. But

NO APOLOGIES

Chanta' fucked around and caught feelings for me when she was doing the exact same damn thing to me. Two heartbroken motherfuckers using each other.

Hearing my phone beep twice indicates I have a new text message. I didn't want to even be bothered by who it was, but I looked at it anyway. **This shit is not cool. I don't appreciate you talking to me just because you miss your precious little Jasmine. When I am around, I should be your focus because if not, then we both can just stop this shit right now!** I took a deep breath, knowing she was right once again, but this woman is draining me. She so stuck on loving Goldie that she was unwilling to love damn near anybody. Guess I have to reply back to this shit. **You right Chanta' I am very sorry. I didn't mean to talk to you like that, come down stairs and we can keep each other company...please.**

Hell! I didn't want to press send but what the hell, it's either deal with her crazy ass, and fuck whenever I want, or go back out and start fucking random bitches again. I don't give a fuck what nobody thinks, there is truly no one like Jasmine; she is definitely one of a kind. Hearing Chanta' come back downstairs, shit my dick start getting hard. She crazy as hell, but her head game is sick. Sitting here in my basketball shorts with no draws on. Fuck! I see her reflection through the T.V. chocolate smooth skin, big ass titties, and small waist; with no stomach and lawd, ass for days. "Derwin, I don't want to argue with you babe."

Chanta' whispered in my ear coming up behind me wrapping her arms around my neck lovingly. I tilted my head back some and smiled. "I don't want to argue either. Chanta' walked in front of me as if I didn't know she was butt ass naked. Fuck! Down boy. I had to tell my dick; didn't want her to see me so damn excited. Now she know damn well, I can't see the Bulls play around all that ass, and she just gonna stand in front of my view. Fuck! Big distraction. "You sure you just wanna watch the game?" Watch this nigga try and lie. His dick just jumping in them damn shorts, and I bet he don't have no damn draws on.

"It's whatever Chanta', you know what you doing. It's cute though." I know how to get this nigga to stop talking crazy; pop a luscious breast in his mouth, he will start sucking like a new born baby. "Well baby let me ride you until we both feel better." Walking up to his ass, and I see nothing but lust in his face. He is staring at a neatly shaved pussy. Climbing on top, with my knees bent with them sinking into the plush burgundy sofa. "Its okay baby, Chanta' is here."

NO APOLOGIES

Feeling his hands caress my shoulders, down my back and over my round ass, as if his hands where made of silk. So gentle, so loving, his lips and hands are covering me like clothes. Feeling his nature rise between my thighs, as my yoni starts to speak to the nature that has come forth to introduce himself. Leaning my head back slightly with closed eyes; letting his hands and mouth explore my body how he sees fit. Nothing but silence can be heard. A choir starts to sing ever so softly in the distance. Our energy is building; heavy breathing is starting, lifting myself up and reaching between my chocolate thighs, I shake hands with nature and guide him home to miss yoni.

NO APOLOGIES

Sliding him in smoothly, makes my body shudder. A moan escapes my lips, as I begin to rotate my hips. I was gripping his nature, and holding him for dear life. His finger tips begin to knead my body, from ass to breast. Grunting with every thrust he throws; matching each other's rhythm. Holding him around his neck, keeping my lips planted deep into his. Our mouths open and let our tongues wrestle for flavor, that we both desired.

Picking up speed; rocking back and forth on his nature. I was feeling it gain more life, as it sits in a familiar space, waiting to paint my walls white. Our moans become smothered, buried in each other's neck as he forcefully flips me and thrust back into me. Our bodies are like waves crashing up against rocks. His hands push down on the top of my ass, while he forcefully thrust back into me. Fuck! This shit is so damn good. Fuck! Why did I let my feelings blind me? This was only suppose to be a fuck buddy thing. He kept his end of the bargain but oh no, I had to go a little deeper. That shit has landed me in a place where I yearn to be with this man fuck!

"That's it Chanta' baby, the way you rocking them hips...fuck...you are going to make me explode," He said. "Explode for momma baby. This dick belongs to me...shit this good dick belongs to me." Man, I would do anything this motherfucker ask me to do, as long as that means he won't be thinking about

NO APOLOGIES

Jasmine ass. It's a damn shame, she got him wide open, and Goldie got me wide open. But we are here fucking each other.

"Ride the fuck out of me Chanta'! Ride me off a cliff, and have me sailing through the clouds to rid my soul of her ass."

"Chanta' is here baby, having you buried inside my home for comfort. Keeping you safe from anyone who can harm you." Fuck! The choir is singing, the marching band is stomping, and cymbals are clanging together. The clouds separate and shine a light of rainbows, through the roof and down on us. "Ouuuuu...shit...Derwin baby...I am...cumminnnnn!" I cried. "Hell yeah, I am about to paint your walls ba...by!" Kissing each other deeply; passionately. This man dick is giving me life. It has resuscitated me. Even for a moment, when I can't stand his ass cause I know most times he be thinking about "Her." I just wish we could have found something in each other, other than this hurricane sex. "Fuck! Chanta' this pussy so fucking good damn; baby!"

"This is your pussy. Baby grind that dick deeper in me. Let these walls take every ounce of juice you got left." Look at this shit. His brows are drawn together, and he biting his bottom lip. Yeah, this motherfucker know good pussy when he in it. But when I hop off this motherfucker's dick, and go wash my ass, he will still be in love his Jasmine. I will still be in love with Goldie. But it is something I really want to talk to him about, and I wonder how will he handle this for god's sake? I hope he don't think I am crazy.

****

Shit, we have been out to get something to eat, just chilling in the house with him, instead of going to my own damn house. This shit feels so right. But I know it's not what he wants. So while we lay in this massive king bed of his, and I may as well say, what the fuck is on my mind and he bet not flip out on me either. "Derwin baaabyyyyy." I figure I'll talk in a soft seductive voice to get his full attention. "Yeah babe what's up?" As usual, he didn't even look at me. He was so fixated on whatever bullshit ass game is on. Literally speaking, I would have to twerk my ass in his face for him to look up at me. He always seems to be in deep thought, but he never says what's on his mind.

Hell! I know he crazy about Jasmine, but damn even I don't think of Goldie ass every minute of the damn day. I snuggle up real close to him, he got the pillow up under his chin resting on it, so I just get as close as I can to him. Maybe if I was naked, no scratch that, then we would be fucking and nothing would be said. That's it, I will just wait until a commercial come on, and offer him a drink. "I will be right back Derwin." A slight nod of the head is what I get. Man this shit gonna have to end. I can't keep living like this with him. But I think that's what I have to say will give him a burst of energy, that he - oh so dearly needs.

With a pair of black booty shorts, and a "Fuck Me Now" black tee-shirt on, I walk to the kitchen down the short hall, and make a quick left. I grabbed two shot glasses, and a bottle of Berry Ciroc. Yup, this should lighten the mood right up. Practically skipping back to the room, this motherfucker may as well be dead. He ain't changed positions, no nothing. "Baby I think we need a drink." Pouring his ass a double shot. I hope this perk him up. "Thanks baby." Well at least he took his glass. "No problem baby, we on chill mode today, so drinks are in order, and you fucked me so good today. I need liquids and food."

I plop down on the bed, swallow my double shot with ease, and began my speech. "Derwin while the game is on commercial can I ask you a quick question?" I asked. "Sure baby go ahead." Derwin sat up, as if he was giving me his full attention at this time. Which I was surprised to see, but he can be attentive at times. I turn around in the bed, and pour both of us another double shot. "O.k. Here it goes, baby we are a mess. You want Jasmine and I want Goldie, but we both feel like we got played by both of them. So I was thinking, since they hurt us. Let's fuck up their supposedly happy home."

Damn! He did not blink, smirk, shake his head; nothing which only means he's thinking, and I am almost scared of what he may say. Especially if he think I have lost my damn mind. "That's your idea, that's what you have been tip toeing around for the last hour for, trying to figure out how to ruin someone else's relationship?"

His tone was low, not even a pitch of excitement ran through him. Fuck I think I just fucked up this plan. "Yes, this is what I have been thinking about.

See people like them, they figure they can do what the fuck they want to folks, and nothing is suppose to be done about it. I say we teach them a fucking lesson."

Derwin came closer to where I was sitting at on the bed, and planted a soft kiss on my full lips. Damn! That shit felt good. He keep on, I am gonna have him put his lips somewhere else. "Brilliant idea baby, just some of the shit that I was thinking to myself for a long while now. I am damn glad to see that I have you on my team. Great minds think alike, and we need to start putting a plan into action now!"

NO APOLOGIES

Now that's more like it. I finally got this man to get excited about something. Now we need to put these great minds together, an come up with a strategy to get things moving. #TeamfuckupJasmineandGoldierelationship.

NO APOLOGIES

Curtis Walker 4

I can't believe I heard that her ass is back in Chicago. She didn't even bother to call me. What the hell is wrong with her? Then again, the only time I do hear from her, is when she having problems with her dude. Shit! Let me stop thinking about this shit before I fuck around and get pissed off. I have been her little secret. This shit is going to have to end. Let me grab my dark blue dress shirt, and black slacks out of the closet, and get myself ready. Before I have to show this house to a woman, who has been trying to book a damn appointment with me for months.

NO APOLOGIES

Man all this fine specimen of a man standing in this mirror, shit! She gonna fuck around and fuck up a good thing. But I be damn if she just start ignoring a motherfucker. I did text her a month ago from an unknown number. Which is what we do to let the other know we wanna talk, then we will call their phone. But my shit went unanswered. It's been ten years I've been fucking with her off and on, and it's time she get her shit together. I have wasted enough of my time. Granted we started out as fuck-buddies, but hell! Over years you catch feelings for people, and you still try and maintain the fuck-buddy status that was put in place earlier.

NO APOLOGIES

Guess at thirty-two, I have played all I can play. It is time I move forward with or without her. Well, depends on if she just saying fuck me, or she just need some time to herself. I will not be thrown to the side for no bitch, not even the fine ass Jasmine Kincaid. I have to get in touch with her some kind of way. Either way, I am about to see her soon. So I hope she ready, cause it's been too long since I had my baby in my arms. To taste the strawberry center of her Paradise is what I am missing.

Just the thought of her ass got my dick brick. I might have to go back in this bedroom, and break Alexis ass off before she get ready to leave too. Alexis; my short stack, 5'5, hourglass body, and old school Toni Braxton haircut. Her ass literally call my name as she walk. I am truly a man who is addicted to the ass. Fuck it. I am practically dressed, and fucking with her will have me late to handle business. Sitting on the edge of my bed, thinking about Alexis and Jasmine, knowing that I would leave Alexis for Jasmine in a heartbeat. So until that shit happens, I need to keep them separate. I don't need no trouble after all, they say - good dick will make a woman lose her mind.

Damn! I wanna call Jasmine, but fuck! I got company, and I am really not in the mood for no bullshit. Hell, if it wasn't for Alexis wanting to suck this dick last night, I would still be in the studio making beats for anyone who's who in the music industry. Hell! They could be just starting out in the rap game and I am still gonna make a beat for them. As long as that money is right. "Alexis baby, it's time to roll you almost ready?"

"Yes I am Curtis, just putting on my heels then we can go." See that's that shit I like, she knows her role. When we done playing, she knows when it's time to go. She don't nag me. She don't ask me no bullshit ass questions all damn day that don't concern her. Hearing her fumble around in the guest bedroom; hoping she kept it the same way she found it. "Alright baby I am ready." Emerging from the guest bedroom was a bomb ass beauty.

NO APOLOGIES

Wearing a red form fitting skirt, with a red and white button up shirt, fitted with a wide black belt that had me almost melt, and the heels, hot damn! She looks like a stallion.

"Damn Alexis, why do you always change in the guest bedroom? All the fucking we do, and you're in here and shit. Makes me think you in here talking to some other dude in my house. She walked her ass up to me, and stood on her tip- toes and planted two soft lips grabbing kisses on me. "Daddy, it's not like that. I just like to be alone when I am getting ready. It's kind of like getting a piece of mind before work." Giving her a light smack on her round ass. "its cool baby...Let's roll."

NO APOLOGIES

Walking out the door; leading her to her car, I gave the enduring forehead kiss, then headed to my car, and watching her drive away. Fuck! I had to rub my damn dick, that woman gives the best fucking head in the world. "Mmmm" That woman got my dick brick hard going into work. I Check myself out in the rearview mirror, make sure my shit together, slide my house music CD in, and roll the fuck to the studio. Damn! Looking up at the sky, it has started raining and shit out here. It's, gonna take about another thirty minutes to get to the studio. Fuck it! I may as well just take my damn time.

NO APOLOGIES

Hell! I don't even know who the fuck these new cats is anyway that I am laying these beats down for. So in the meantime; cruise with my house music and make another phone call. **Ring... Ring... Ring..."You know who you have called so at the beep leave a message." "Hey baby it's me we need to get up...One."** Ain't this some shit? ...Deep sigh... I don't understand why I even put up with this shit. Bending blocks in the rain, getting my thoughts together... **Screech!** Fuck! I slam on breaks. Why in the hell am I looking at Alexis car on this side of town? Her ass suppose to be at work and shit; license plate read **"BADD BTCH."** So I know she can't deny this shit...Thank god for smart phones. These motherfuckers don't lie. With a quick snap of my camera I got this hoe.

NO APOLOGIES

Alexis 5

"Alexis girl, what the fuck you doing strolling up in here today?" With a pop of my lips, as if I just took a sour lollipop out of my mouth. I answered with a roll of my neck. "Ewww, why you all up in my damn business Jerome? I come and go where I please, and this is where I want to be. You know better about asking grown folks questions!"

"Don't get nasty Ms. Thang, I just know you suppose to be at work, and not up in my shop. So with that damn attitude, why don't you just take your little hot shit ass on back to that high end ass salon you work at, and leave the slumming to us." Man, I sure do know how to ruffle Jerome feathers.

NO APOLOGIES

He always tripping on me. Ever since I stopped doing hair up in his shop, and started working Downtown. I met Curtis one-day at Starbucks, and told him I could line him up just a little bit better. Next thing I know, I was at his home with his dick in my mouth. I am now working in an upscale salon.

Hell for all I know he fucking the owner, but hey as long as he fucking me too, and passing that damn money my way, he can do whatever he wants as long as he don't fuck over me. Looking around the shop, this shit hasn't changed much in the last year. Same two wash bowls, his mommas old as couch in the so called waiting area; which is really the left side of the entrance as you walk in.

NO APOLOGIES

Flat screen on the wall playing what; porn. Hair all on the floor, and him and Ms. Jaki sharing insults as always. Oh, let me not forget the two stylist chairs that Charles ass tries to run, but I wasn't having that shit. Keep your ass in your lane, I will do the same. Jerome ass can smoke some hair tho, he will lay it, dye it, and fry it to the side. Meeting him was funny.

When I took a much needed vacation to New Orleans, I saw him on Bourbon street cat calling every fine ass man he saw, not necessarily for a good time. After he came out the closet to his family, they kicked his ass out and he was fucking for money just to survive. But he was hooking up some damn hair along the way. We both on Bourbon Street acting a fool, making cat calls and getting cat calls. When I told him I was from Chicago, he really wanted to come back with me, and as they say the rest is history. "Man Jerome ain't nobody got time to hear what you saying today! Hey Ms. Jaki, looking good girl."

"You know you my boo Alexis," Jerome grinning all big and shit trying to win me over with that smile. "Man! Put those thirty-twos away, while I hang up my jacket."

Pulling a chair out the back-room; which is the stock room, break room, and sometimes fuck room. I wouldn't change Jerome for no one in the world. We know each other's secrets and shit, and I love his Nawlins' accent. I could talk to him all day, just to hear him talk. I would never tell him that shit though. It may go to his head.

"Alright Ms. Hot Shit, where is that fine ass man at you fucking? Can you believe her ass Jacki, she leaves us for him. I can't believe this shit! So spill it I know you got some drama to tell." Look at these two, always trying to hit me up for information when it come to my relationships. Jerome sitting here with his hand across his forehead like he got fever or something, and Ms. Jaki being his amen corner. These two are ridiculous. After clearing my throat, while they looked at me intensely. I almost didn't want to speak but what the hell.

"If you two hens must know, yes me and Curtis is just fine. Yes we fuck every chance we get. Yes he has fucked me in the ass. Yes I have swallowed his nut, and yes I hope to be moving in with him soon." These heffas looking at me like I said something wrong. "Why y'all looking at me like that?" I asked. "We know all that Ms. Thang, hell you stay horny...We want to know has he fucked up yet?" No Jerome didn't ask me no shit like that. "Fuck y'all!" I shouted with an attitude.

"Don't get mad at us, hell we just asked a question. And since when do you trip out on us for saying some shit like that?" Jerome asked. "That was a fucked up question you asked Jerome damn!" I saw Jaki gathering her things. Every time Jerome and I get into a heated debate, she always take off running like a bat out of hell. So I just had to ask her why she was leaving. "Umm Jaki you look like you just got here and now you are leaving. What's up with that?"

"Well if you must know Ms. Thang I am running out to get some breakfast for all of us and let you and Jerome have y'all little talk." Damn! She gave me two snaps and a circle, grabbed her purse, and sashayed on up outta the salon. I looked at Charles knowing we was about to finish this conversation.

NO APOLOGIES

"Jerome…" What the hell did he just cut me off? I am in mid stride to ask him something, and Jaki ass interrupts as always. "Wait Alexis, we joke like this a lot. I didn't realize that he meant so much to you. I mean after all, you are still sleeping with other people. Not throwing shade, but I am stating the facts."

Jerome watched me intensely, knowing that he can read me like a fucking book. I didn't mean to snap on him, but damn it! I don't need the jokes right now, when it comes to a man that I am seriously in love with. "It's cool Jerome. I should have told you how I really felt about him, instead of acting like it was nothing, but I just didn't want to get to close to fast. Hell, we both know how that story usually turns out." Sharing a laugh with him was good. All he wants for me is to be happy, and all I want for him is to be happy.

"Well Ms. Alexis. Do what you will; with whomever you want. I want you happy, and if you happy, I am happy. Gurl, in this life, we live. None of us are promised tomorrow, so we all should be doing what makes us happy." No words formed, but the buzzing of my cell phone going off rapidly in my damn Vince Camuto purse. It was driving me insane. I tried to ignore it earlier, but damn! I am trying to talk shit with Jerome. Guess I gotta answer it damn! Pulling my phone out, I see it is five missed texted messages. Who the fuck wants me that damn bad? Why they blowing me up in a text, and won't call.

Unlocking my screen, who do I see? Curtis ass blowing me back to back practically. First text: **Where are you?** Second text: **Call me as soon as you get this message.** Third text: **See that's why I don't do relationships. Nobody can keep it one hundred.** Fourth text: **Where are you?** Fifth text: **I am trying to keep calm, but you are making it very damn difficult to do so!** Oh shit! Let me call his ass right now. He done lost his damn mind, and I don't have time for no bullshit. See, just like a man; you don't answer him right back, he lose his damn mind. He will never say it, but hell, when pussy talks it can fuck up a man's mind.

"Jerome excuse me. I am about to step in the back and make a phone call." I briefly said. "It's cool boo I gotta get ready for my next client anyway." I step my ass in the back, look through my call log and find his name and press call. **Ring... Ring... Ring... "You have reached Curtis leave me a message." "Hey baby, I am returning your call, my phone was in my purse and I didn't hear it. I will call you back a little later...Oh, and call next time instead of all these damn text messages."**

I didn't even wait for the beep. I just hung the fuck up. The nerve of his ass texting me with that crazy shit, then don't answer. Man, I don't have time to fuss and fight tonight. This is a clear indication that I need to take my ass to my own damn apartment tonight. "You alright Ms. Thang? You go in the back smiling now you look like you are ready to chew nails."

"Man Jerome, I get a fucking text from Curtis and then when I call, he don't even answer. He do this shit to me the entire fucking time blow me up and then when I reach out to him by calling. He don't even answer." Is his ass smirking at me, as I talk what the hell is so damn funny? "Ummm. Why are you smiling and shit, Jerome?" I asked. "I am smiling at your ass, gurl please, he text you and shit have you return his call, and then he not answer.

Why didn't you just text him back? Hell you and I

both know he wasn't gonna answer because he

pissed. He do it all the time. Next time unless he

call you, I wouldn't return shit for that simple

reason...Yup I am petty, so what."

Jerome can be very damn petty, but he always

have a point. Curtis does this shit all the damn time.

He will text, and when I call, he won't answer. Hell!

He probably only do that shit to pull me away. From

whatever he thinks is holding my attention. "Yeah.

You are right Jerome. He do this shit every time,

and then I am the one sitting here with the

attitude. I have already told myself that I am going

to my own damn house tonight. I don't want to have to argue with him tonight." Jerome, nodding his head in approval, made me smile. No matter what, I know he got my damn back.

"Well Jerome luv, I am gonna get out of your hair. I know you got work to do, and all this beauty is nothing but a damn distraction for your ass." We both laughed out loud at my statement, which it happens to be true. "Biotch please! Maybe before but now, no way. Anyway, this client I got coming in here, she gets on my damn nerves, so please stay. Especially if you don't have work your damn self. You can stay here and kick it with me until I am done. Then we can go get some Margaritas."

NO APOLOGIES

I guess he was right. When I am usually off, I either go shopping or to the shop, and do walk-ins, but not today. I will hang with my family. "Oh shit, here comes Queen Bitch now." Jerome was looking through the blinds when he said that, and started shaking his head. Damn! When she walked in, I saw a bad ass body. It's like her body was designed in a factory. She look like she was moving in slow motion, coming through the damn door. Long ringlets of jet black hair; shit her hair didn't even look like it needed to be done, but whoever she is, she is one bad mother fucker.

NO APOLOGIES

`INDIGO 6

Every single time I come on this side of town, I be ready to pass out, and the hood is not where I want to be, but damn it! If Charles didn't smoke some weave. I wouldn't even be here. I am gonna have to see if I can get him to buy, or rent some property in a better neighborhood. My Real Estate license not only got me more shit than them dicks I was with, but I am able to help folks like Jerome move from the hood to a better place. Shit! I thought when I was done with Goldie, it was a done deal, but after seeing Jasmine ass at the store not too long ago; lawd that shit sparked my interest with Goldie ass again.

NO APOLOGIES

Knowing damn well it shouldn't, but if anyone know good dick, like I know good dick, that nigga right there got some good ass dick. I bet she don't even know what to do with that motherfucker either. Shit! Just thinking about his ass, got my pussy doing the percolator. Let me shake this shit off my mind and get my ass on to this shop before I make a fucking phone call or some shit. Walking up in the beauty shop, immediately to my left was that ratty ass couch. I told him he needs to put some chairs in here or something. What the fuck, this shit is so damn ghetto. "Hey Jerome hunny." We give air kisses like we always do, and air hugs. He is a real cool person, but damn! I don't need to be hugging every damn person I am cool with.

NO APOLOGIES

"Heyyyy Biotch!" He greets me with the two snaps and head twirl.

Jerome ass is so fucking entertaining. "Jerome, this gonna be my last damn time coming down here. You need to think about getting you another place. You are no longer the kitchen beautician. Your ass need to be right downtown where the rich bitches at." His eyes lit up because he knows I am right. I am a bitch this I know, but I know my shit when it comes to business. A gay man in the downtown area of Chicago, whipping up folks hair is hot shit. "Don't start that shit Indigo. I love hanging with my people down here, and we are just fine."

NO APOLOGIES

"Girlfriend, would you tell his ass it's time to upgrade. Hell, he can smoke some hair and he damn sho' don't charge like he for the people. I am sorry. I'm Indigo and you are?" "I'm Alexis, me and Jerome go back a long way. And I must admit it Jerome, she ain't telling you nothing the rest of us haven't said already. It's time to up- grade baby," She said. "See finally, someone around here agrees with me." Damn! Got me wailing my arms in the air. It's like Jerome don't get it. Fuck this ghetto shit out here! Go somewhere; where your skills will truly be recognized. This shit makes no sense to me, and apparently it don't make sense to Alexis either.

NO APOLOGIES

"Y'all bitches getting on my damn nerves. I will think about it, and let y'all know what I think. So in the meantime, in between time, Indigo get your ass over here so I can rock this hair gurl." **SMACK!** Every time his ass speak, he always gotta smack his damn lips. Especially when he serious about something. "While you smacking them damn lips of yours, let's get started on my damn hair. I really don't have all damn day to be up in here."

"Ummm. No the fuck you didn't miss thang, gonna **TRY** and rush me in my own damn shop; the nerve of motherfuckers." **SMACK** "Okay Jerome, as long as you please stop smacking, and do some work we will be good." Got my hell to the nawl woman stance on; hands on hips, applying weight on one leg, and neck rolling. Hell, He ain't gonna be smacking his lips too many more times. His smack is the same as my neck roll. It's ghetto for, 'I am not playing with your ass.'

Walking my ass over to the hair chair, Jerome starts to take my damn weave out and I ask this other woman, who was she? I don't give two fucks I like to know the kind of people I am around just in case I gotta open a can of whoop ass on someone. Hell! These motherfuckers be fooled by the red bottoms. Like I won't go in on their asses. So while Jerome is working his magic, I get in this woman's business real damn quick. "Well Alexis, are you and

Jerome from the same parts of town and what not?" I asked. "Yes you can say that." I can't believe this chick all up in my business. That shit may fly with these motherfuckers, who don't mind her all in their shit, but being from the Chi, we don't get down like that. We mind our own fucking business. Unless someone gives up information, then we speak on it. Hell! Even then you got to be careful shit...motherfuckers are sensitive about certain shit.

"Okaaay, I see we are a little uneasy about folks asking you questions," I smiled in at her letting her know all is good. Did this bitch just say uneasy? No I am not uneasy. I just don't like to display all my shit to folks I just fucking met...This bitch Indigo is a trip. I got to ask Jerome how in the hell did he come across a woman like this? "Excuse me Indie it's not tha...." Does this bitch think she's about to get another word in, after calling me by the wrong damn name? This bitch know my name. Once it is said, it can never be forgotten. "Hold the hell on." Hell, I had to take a deep breath on that one. I had to sit the hell up straight in the damn hair chair.

"Do you think I am gonna let you skip by, and keep right on talking, after calling me by the damn wrong name. Please! Let's not start no shit, but I will say it for you one more time, my name is Indigo." Aww shit, I see I got a bitch ready to cut a motherfucker. Okay, let me read this motherfucker one more time, so she know I am not the one who she wants to be fucking with. "Well, Ms. Indigo you can do what you please, and rock how you like, but don't come for me unless your ass is looking for a fucking fight!" I didn't even get up and do my ghetto girl stance, this bitch must be crazy if she think she can talk to me any ol' kind of way. This is not that.

I don't see how Jerome deals with this bullshit, and clearly she on some bullshit today. "Now, now ladies please! Calm all that noise down, both of you are my road dogs but I can't have all this negative energy up in my shop. I need positive energy, and tranquility in my life, and y'all bitches fucking it up in here!" Jerome doing his neck roll with every damn word he speaks, like either one of us really give a fuck what he talking about. All I know, he better check his friend before I have to continue to check her my damn self. "Well I see Ms. Alexis got some bite in her I like it." Did this chick just smile while saying that shit? Oh! Not only is she a bitch, but she a crazy bitch and I simply don't have the time. Gathering my things, I told Jerome I would meet him at our spot for drinks later, and let him have time with Ms. INDIGO. Walking out the door; keys in hand, purse on shoulder. Now I gotta go find out what the hell is up with Curtis ass.

Yup, mixing the old with the new.

No telling how this shit gonna turn

out. But don't be too ready to

judge, everyone ain't what/who

they seem(ed) to be.

Fast forward six weeks later.

Jasmine 7

"Damn baby you truly know how to eat some pussy shit!" His ass is gonna make me tap out in two seconds. The fucking room is spinning, I have squirted and came more times than I can remember. I truly believe his ass is trying to kill me with his head game. What the fuck is he doing to me? **"Slurrrrpppppp" "Slurrrrpppppp"** Fuck! I am ready to just fuck, now this motherfucker done drew figure eights; spelled the alphabet, and spelled his name. If I tremble one mo' damn time, I am gonna pass out. "Hold on baby....fuck....you eating this pussy too damn good I can hardly catch my fucking breath."

NO APOLOGIES

Just as I said that, he started again, and have the nerve to be looking at me the whole time. Watching him suck on my clit, is about to make the volcanic pussy erupt again. Damn! He flicking his tongue fast with purpose, and determination. Oh damn! He's starting to shake his head side to side, and up and down. Fuck! My clit is swollen. Shit! There goes his two fingers deep inside Paradise, telling me to come here again. Fuck! I don't want to cum here again, but he is commanding that I do. Fuck! This pussy can never say no to him. Shit a tongue like his is a gift, and a curse.

I have been laying here for a little over an hour, getting my pussy tongued fucked; fingered fucked, sucked, licked, and nibbled on. "Baby I am about to cum again...Oh fuck! Get all my juices, suck on this pussy! Fuuuccckkk!" Twirling my hips on his tongue, like a Professional Jamaican dancer. His hands are scooped under my ass holding me in place while my legs are resting on his shoulders. Damn! all I see is twinkling dots above my head. What kind of shit is this? I am gonna have to stop this shit. I literally feel like my damn head is about to explode. Even when he stop licking and sucking. It still feel like he is. The power of this man's tongue game is fucking outrageous.

"You want me to stop babe...let you catch your breath... or should I keep going real slow?" See what I mean he knows I want him to stop but damn it I don't want him to stop. "Yes...baby...let me catch my breath." Fuck! I feel like I have just ran a 5k marathon. "No problem baby. Catch your breath while I run to the bathroom, but keep them legs open just like that till I get back." I came so damn much, I don't want to even have sex now. I have squirted all over the damn place. The bed is soaked though; damn near. I really should be putting on my damn clothes. Hell! I gotta hide the pussy from this motherfucka.

Just as I was sitting up in the bed...damn here he comes again. "Are you trying to get away from me baby?" he asked. "Curtis, you are about to kill a sistah. I already cannot breathe and you trying to do more to me." Rubbing my hand across my damn throat, and on the other hand, across my chest. It's like every time I cum, it is equivalent to someone cutting off your oxygen, then giving it back just as you are gasping for air. My damn hair is all over my head, and this beast of a man is standing in front of me; with a chiseled body, and a hard dick that could knock down a fucking building. Looking up at him; biting on my bottom lip, watching him walk closer.

I feel like I am cemented to the bed. What he is about to do is epic as always. He never does anything any other way. "Come here Jazzi, slide your beautiful body towards the end the bed, and lay on your stomach." Oh damn! What the fuck is he about to do? I can't take this man. He makes sure no matter what, he stays a constant reminder in my mind. Burying any thoughts of anyone else who may be lingering around in there. Laying on my stomach, after I scoot to the edge of the bed, I feel him walk up behind me. That fine baby hair on the back of my neck stands up, just because I feel him near me so close.

I feel his legs separate my legs. He leans on me kissing, and licking my neck. Sending a warm tongue trailing down my spine. Letting the air hit the wet spot that sends chills through my body, has my nipples stand at attention more than ever. I feel his tongue slide in between my ass. Before he separates my ass cheeks with his hands, and dart his stiff tongue in and out of my asshole. Grinding on his tongue, I feel him kneel down, so my legs can fall on top of his shoulders. Slowly he picks me up, upside down. I grab on to his waist and lock my legs around his neck, while he starts to eat my pussy again. Lawd have mercy! This motherfucka will eat my pussy in any way he can. I just love his way of thinking. Deep throating him; the room is filled with moans, "ohhs" and "ahhs" every few seconds.

Slow strokes, as he continue to taste all of me. This man gives eating pussy a whole new meaning. Because I am sucking his dick, I don't have to worry about a headache hanging upside down like this. "Aaahhhh fuck! I feel another cum coming on...shit!" This man is going to drain the fuck out of me. I ain't going to be no good for no one else. Body is starting to tremble; holding his waist tighter. It's time for him to let me down. Before I could use the safe word we picked out, he started walking to the bed to let me down.

Sliding back on the bed, he is keeping is mouth suctioned to my pussy. The whole damn time; licking back up the crack of my ass, up my spine and then my neck. In one swift motion, he slides his blessing inside of me. "**GASP!**" "I am gonna go slow baby don't worry...Mmmmmm." His words bounced in my ear, through my brain, and traveled through the rest of my body. His words made a home inside of me, where he could never be evicted. "I know you will baby...I know you will," softly I whisper back.

Feeling him slide in and out of me with ease; long deep strokes and short pauses, as he is deep in me. Letting my pussy expand for his girth. His hands form around my waist; slightly hiking my ass up, sliding in and out of me. "Ahhh fuck...Jazzi...I missed this pussy. I feel this pussy opening up for me you know I like this shit!" He exclaimed passionately. "I know you do baby...fuck! You deep in this pussy Curtis!" As soon as I say that, his ass start to speed up and go in on my pussy. Fuck! His strokes is now short, and quick hard thrusts.

This man is gonna fuck me into a coma. Ass slapping, hair pulling, biting, scratching, and the ultimate neck grabbing. He's squeezing tight enough where I am so turned the fuck on right now, but not enough to where I can't breathe. "You like this shit baby? Fuck! I have missed you so much Jazzi, damn! I want you to cream all on this dick for daddy," he said. "I am going to cream daddy...I am about to cream daddddyyyyy!" Creaming all over his dick, fuck! I am out for the count. Feeling him pound into me over and over. His ass is fucking with great   determination.   **THRUST… THRUST…**

THRUST… THRUST…

"Ohh…fuck Jazzi! That's that shit right there. Keep squeezing this dick baby. Yes, like that fuck baby…fuck…fuck…fuckkkkkkkkkkk!" Shit! He is about to explode. "Lay that shit on my tongue baby. Damn! Give me that sweetness!" I jag and lick the underside of the head. Repeatedly, until an explosion comes and coats my tongue. He grabs a fist full of hair, sliding my head back and forth, as the last bit of soul leaves his body. We slowly collapse onto the bed, breathing, heaving; three hours of pure fucking and sucking. I swear, I am gonna be walking out of this hotel like I have been riding a horse all my damn life.

"Damn baby don't stay gone like that again I have missed you like crazy Jazzi I need you baby." Hearing him whisper those words into my ear was pure heaven. It is always a good feeling when someone wants you, and needs you in their world. No matter how much he wants or needs me, my heart belongs to Goldie, and there is no changing that shit.

Curtis 8

Thinking back to when I met Jasmine, she was on her way to NYC to attend college. She seemed to be having a not so good day, when I saw her at Fatty's Soul Food Restaurant. I was coming home from laying some tracks down, and I was dead ass tired. Looking for a quick bite to eat before I head home, as always, the joint was packed with late night party goers. Seeing I had number 17 and, they were on number 10, irritated the fuck out of me. Instantly shaking my head, I headed over to the only table that had one person sitting at it. She was gorgeous. A little young looking for me, but never the less I was smitten from the start.

NO APOLOGIES

"Do you mind if I sit here, and wait for my order to be called?" I asked. Really hoping she would say yes, but as tired as I was, I didn't really care what she would say I was sitting regardless. "No, have a seat." Her voice was soft, no drama or bullshit attached to it. "How long have you been waiting beautiful?" I asked. "Oh, I am not waiting. I am just sitting here thinking." Now when she said thinking, I must admit, what could someone so damn pretty have to worry about, so damn late at night? "If you don't mind me saying, whatever he did, don't sweat it. Let him keep fucking up until someone else show you how it's done." When she saw the look of discernment in my face, her face lit up like a Christmas tree.

"How do you know it's about a man?" I smiled knowing I was reeling in my bait. "For starters, you are up in a damn restaurant at 3 a.m. on a Saturday, instead of being on your way home with your man, or to your man. Then you didn't even order anything. Which means possible loss of appetite. So yes, I think it is safe to say it's about a man." Her smile at that very moment lit my insides up. Now here I am, a twenty year old man laying tracks down for whoever, whenever I can. I am making a good living. I had women I was fucking daily and nightly, no kids, and no bullshit.

NO APOLOGIES

Just money and pussy. Looking at her made me want to put her on my team. Sitting there talking until my order came up, I learned that she was going to college to become an Author; that we are sitting in her aunts restaurant, she has no kids, and is in love with a man who wants to have his cake and eat it too. At that very moment, I should have walked away and never looked back, but before I left with my order, I gave her my number just in case she needed someone to talk to. One month later, she called. I didn't know who the fuck it was, so I let the call go to voicemail. The phone rang again so I answered. "Hello."

NO APOLOGIES

"Well you finally picked up huh?" She said. "Only because you called twice, but I would never forget the sound of your voice Jazzi." I playfully retorted. "Oh! Pet names already?" She said. "A cute name, for a cute girl. Damn! Took you long enough to call a brotha. I thought you threw the damn number out, or simply was not interested." I heard her chuckle over the phone; sounded real cute. "Oh, I was interested from the moment I saw you walk in the restaurant, but I am just settling in at school first. So how have things been going in your world?"

Actually, I have been doing well dropping beats for some new folks. Doing what I do," I said. "I was wondering, if you are not busy this weekend, would you like to come check me out in NYC?" Oh shit! Look at her inviting me down, so we can get down. Hell cause I know she don't think I coming to twiddle my damn thumbs. But she so damn cute. I may have to take a pass just to keep her around. She still stuck on her dude, so we gonna see how this shit play out. Does she think I am going to be a side dude, or does she want more?

"Well, I can clear my calendar for you baby. Let me know what day you want me to come down there, and I will make the arrangements. Now I hope you don't think that I am going to come down there just to watch NYC traffic." Hell! I was trying to give her a damn hint to let her know that I will be on fuck mode. But I see she want to play this little come and get me game, so fuck it! I will be there. "I don't have classes this Friday, and I have a late class on Monday, so can you come down Friday morning?" She asked.

"I will be there by noon on Friday, but wait don't you live in the dorms?" Hell, I damn sho ain't gonna be on fucking in nobodies dorm room. I am a freak but umm, no I will pass. "No, I have a small apartment that I rent out, so whenever I want to have a party, or just want some me time, I go there on the weekends," she said. "Okay then, I will see you in a few days around noon Jazzi. Oh, I am glad you called." Now I am all smiles and shit, but still cool. I guess because I know she has a man, but yet she wants me at least for the weekend. I just hope ol' boy and I, never cross paths. I won't fight over no pussy, but I will kick a niggas ass for stepping to me the wrong way. Bullshit ain't bout nothing, but I do know how niggas get over pussy and a pretty face. "Talk to you soon."

I can't believe I am in NYC for a chick. Man, my boys will clown my ass, if they knew this shit. Hey, what they don't know, They can't clown me for. One bag packed; a couple pairs of jeans, shirts and draws, and I keep the crispy Nike joints on deck. She has texted me, gave me the address and everything already. I just landed thirty minutes ago; hopping in a yellow cab, shouting from the back seat, giving him the address, looking out the window. The fucking streets was crowded as hell.

It was wall to wall people on the streets, and the cars was bumper to bumper. This shit is crazy! I will take the Dan Ryan back in Chicago any day. This motherfucking cab swerving hard, and shit. I mean I know he know the streets and what not, but damn he can slow down. Slapping that cabbie a dub I took out, I got out and slammed the door. I wanted to cuss him out for driving so damn reckless, but damn it! I am on a mission right now, and hell!

NO APOLOGIES

Everyone knows that when pussy talks most guys

listen.

Goldie 9

Damn baby! This is my third time texting you. Umm you need to hit me now! I bet that's my last damn time texting her ass, and she wonder why I am always suspicious of her ass all of a sudden. She done got real motherfucking sneaky and shit. Always saying she with her girls. She need girl time and shit. What the hell she need is to be here with me and Rasheeda. I can't believe this shit! I am in the house, and now she out. This shit has been going on for weeks. I bet I put a stop to this shit as soon as she get home. As soon as I pick my phone up, it chimes letting me know I got a text. Damn near dropped the fucking phone trying to see who texted me.

Hey baby, I just saw your message. I will be home in five minutes, coming around the corner now. Five minutes. Yeah we gonna see as soon as she walks in. Got me sitting my ass on the couch, bouncing one leg like a fucking crack head with a drink in my hand, and it's only nine at night. Man, when I heard the fucking keys, I sprang up from the couch, and was on beast mode. When she entered the corridor, it took everything in me not to start cussing her ass out. I stood at the entrance watching her every move like a fucking hawk. The way she hung her jacket up, kicked off her fuck me pumps, laid her purse down on the navy blue chair beside the coat rack, which was immediately to the left as you walked through the door.

"Hey babe." Did she just throw the "Hey babe" at me like it was nothing and she's been gone practically all damn day? "Hey baby, where the hell you been?" I wanted to cuss her ass out right then and there, but I'll wait and see how this thing gonna play out first. "Since when did you start questioning me about my whereabouts?" She asked. "When I sensed you been lying to me about where the fuck you been!" Okay, I gotta stay calm because the shit that is running through my mind, makes me see how motherfuckers can end up on the First 48. This will not be a whole night of Q&A, either she going to be honest or she gonna keep lying and then that's where we are going to have a big problem.

"I was with friends having a few cocktails, and now I am home. What the hell is wrong with you tonight?" She retorted. "There is not a damn thing wrong with me, but there will be something wrong with you, if you don't start telling me the fucking truth around here." I kept my tone cool, nice and low but stern. The look on her face told me she knew I wasn't playing, but she was gonna hold true to her story since I already know she lying. Got me following up behind her ass around the house; from bathroom to bedroom, like some fucking puppy dog. Watching her ass from the back she even walking different. It is taking everything in me, not to snatch her the fuck up. I promised her I wouldn't lay hands on her anymore, but my fucking blood is boiling within me and I am on edge.

"Okay Jas," I clasped my hands together, sitting on the bed watching her every move. Normally she would get naked and sashay her bubble ass to the bathroom, but tonight she grabbed her robe and house slippers, and went into the bathroom without even taking her clothes off. See this ain't shit new to me. I know the signs to look for, but the fact that she think I don't know the game because a nigga all in love, makes her look like the damn fool. "Okay Jas, what?" She asked. "I am going to ask you one more time where were you, and before you say with your girls, please remember Jas, this is **GOLDIE** you talking to," I smirked as I finished my sentence. Looking at her as hesitation grew on her face, then she became fidgety with her hands.

"I have to take a shower and lay down. I am just tired and you are bombarding me with these bullshit ass questions. For the last time I was with my girls having drinks." Off to the bathroom she went thinking she was leaving me on dummy. Well the joke is on her ass. I will not now or not ever, play the dummy for no motherfucka including her ass. If I stay in, we are going to argue all damn night.

NO APOLOGIES

If I go out, I may fuck around and fuck someone. Fuck it! I will stay in just so she don't think I am doing the tit for tat thing, but I am damn close to doing so. That's why it doesn't pay to try to be on the straight and narrow. Muthafuckas still try you because they think you are on the same old bullshit you used to be on. I guess I will be taking my ass in the other room tonight. She knows, I know she has fucked up, and I am gonna let her sweat. Reaching over to grab my phone off of the glass coffee table, I give her one last look before she turns, and heads for the bathroom.

Grabbing the remote; watching whatever sports is on television, my mind is racing like a muthafucka. I know the old saying "what is done in the dark will come to the light," I knew this day was going to come. I just didn't know when, and I am just glad that I was prepared for it. Flicking on the T.V. like a mad man; trying to cover my thoughts with the news, when in actuality, all I can think about is going in that fucking bedroom and fucking her until she fucking passes out. But I am a nigga from the streets, fucking behind another nigga ain't my style.

It would be different if I didn't know about it, but damn it! I know, and I am really trying to see how to handle this shit. Either leave it alone, let her do her until she get it out her system, or let her know

I know, and then give her an ultimatum. Fuck this!

I know what I am about to do. **Ring… Ring… Ring…**

"Hello."

"Hey ma," I said. "Umm, who the hell is this on my fucking line?" She asked. "Girl please! If you don't stop playing with me. You may forget many other niggas, but I'm one nigga you will never forget." Look at this shit, now she wanna play like she don't know who the fuck I am. I swear, I don't know why most of these women playing these dumb ass games with me tonight. "You know what ma? Never mind that I called. See you lost your fucking memory…deuces." That's it. I am staying my ass home before I fucking hurt somebody. What the fuck is this, fuck up Goldie's day or what? Bitches lying, and getting on my damn nerves. Man, I must be turning soft because this shit right here would not even be a question on whether to go off or not. I would be going off and out the fucking door by now.

Some of the shit... I wonder who the fuck is this texting me, looking over at my phone, seeing a blue light keep blinking, has thrown off my thought process. Checking my damn phone, and this shit like to pissed me off immediately. **Yeah Goldie, I know this was your ass. I haven't heard from in a long while, so why are you really texting me? Aren't you at home with little miss wifey?** Look at this dumb shit. If she didn't want to speak, why the hell text me? She know, out of all women, that I am not about to chase no ass. Especially if that's all you are to me. Throwing my phone back on the bed wondering, thinking, and planning, as always.

A slight tap on the door, and in walks Jas. With a damn towel wrapped around her body, hair dangling in her face, and the faint scent of some chocolate shit she puts on, filled the air. "Hey baby, I didn't know if you were sleep or not. Are you planning on coming to bed anytime soon?" she inquired. "Later maybe... why... what's up?" I replied. "I just thought we could lay together that's all babe." She always do this dumb shit. Know I am mad, then walks her ass in here like ain't nothing wrong. She always pull the sex card on me as much of a nigga as I am. She done played the wrong damn card tonight. The thought of fucking behind some nigga is fucking me up, and bout to have me fuck her up.

"You know what Jas? As much as I would love to have you lay next to me, under better circumstances would be fine. But under this bullshit ass circumstance, its best you take your ass in the bedroom and get some sleep. I will see you in the morning, and close the door on your way out." I continued clicking on the T.V. as if I was looking for something, knowing damn well I wasn't.

NO APOLOGIES

Watching her standing in front of me with her towel wrapped around her, and her mouth gapping open in pure shock. Let me further know she on some bullshit. Then she walked out the room just as quietly as she came in, and closed the damn door.

Indigo 10

I can't believe this nigga calling and shit, like I am suppose to just jump up and answer for him. He may have some fools in his life, but damn it! I will not be one of them. I mean, I did text him to let him know that I knew it was him calling all along, but seriously, what could he want at night time other than some pussy? On top of that, his ass got in house pussy. So he really needs to lose my number. Besides I have a new man, and he treats me just right. I don't have no time for this bullshit with Goldie ass.

Knowing him, he's either pissed about something, or just being the dog ass nigga he is, and just want to fuck someone. His reason for calling me, could only mean that. He never wanted anything else with me other than a sexual relationship but this pussy is getting dicked down by a monster dick that knows how to please me and take care of my needs; not that I asked him to, but he came correct from the very beginning. Living downtown in a loft is amazing; I can look over and see Lake Michigan.

I don't have to worry about the bullshit that comes with home repairs. For the most part, all the old niggas I was fucking with, I no longer wanted them be able to just come by whenever the spirit moved them. I needed a fresh start, I wanted to be able to just leave the bullshit behind, and start anew, and that meant getting a new place to live. Walking around this loft daily, as my feet become familiar with the wooden floors; the ceramic counter tiles in the kitchen, the Jacuzzi and stand up six shower head in the bathroom and my massive California King bed, I feel alive here. There is an old saying "The quickest way to get over a man is get under a new man," and damn it! They did not lie.

I am woman enough to admit that I did fall in love with Goldie's no good ass. As much dick as I got elsewhere, I still couldn't shake him, I tried my damnedest to shake his ass, but I couldn't. Goldie has this magnetic appeal about him from the way he dress, the low tone of his voice, and the way he commands attention and respect just by entering a room. The fucked up thing about that is, he creeps in your brain by telling you all the good shit you want to hear; giving you some of that good dick, and even when he says he don't want a woman he makes you feel like you are his woman. Then you see his ass with some other woman twenty-four hours later, and get instantly pissed.

I start remembering how he held me, kissed me, sucked every inch of my body. Whispering in my ear, telling me he loves me. That man, that man! Every time I think about his ass, my fucking body starts to shudder with excitement, and panties start to slowly get creamed. It should be against the fucking law on how one man can have this much power over any woman. Hell! Every woman that he has probably come across, I am sure he has left a cemented foot print in their hearts. He finally went legit with his mentoring program. From what I hear on the streets, it is thriving.

He goes by his government name now, instead of his street name Goldie, I must admit he is really trying to do his legit thing. I will never forget how he treats women just to serve as a pawn in his bullshit ass games. I can say one more thing about Goldie, he is one of the few men that will tell you the truth about something, but that shit don't mean shit really, when feelings get involved.

It's Vodka and cranberry juice time. I haven't heard from my monster dick, so I guess I will rest my pussy tonight. Because when he does call, he don't want to hear shit about my pussy being sore from the last time we were together. Now, this man is definitely someone who will get me to get over Goldie ass. I am not like most women I don't sit around and wait for Mr. Right to come and get me or just fall in my lap. I go get his ass, and fuck up his whole understanding with this pussy and head game. Shit, I love the fact that I got the bomb ass pussy. I don't need to broadcast. I have brains and booty too. If I want to deal with you on that level, then I will let you into my brain world. If we just fucking; no need to get to know each other on an intellectual level, and no need for faking shit.

Women call me a bitch, ho, and a home-wrecker. None of that shit matters to me, but a bitch will never be able to call me a fake hoe. My monster dick has told me he has a woman that he is really feeling, and that's all good since I am in no way wanting to be anyone's woman right now. I just got my new loft. I am doing me the best way I know how and I am fucking and having a ball. **BEEP...** Hearing my damn phone beep, I can hope it is not Goldie ass texting me again. I don't want to end up in his fucking bed again. Almost scared to look at the damn text, I reach over on my glass coffee table to see who texted me.

Hey baby, thinking about that sweet ass pussy! Aww, shit! He's thinking about this pussy, and probably laid the fuck up with his boo. I may be a bitch, but damn it! When you got it, you got it. Crossed legs on my cream sofa, drink in hand and R. Kelly singing through the house, I am surely gonna text him back. He knows where the good-good is at. **Baby you know where this good pussy is at. When you are ready for it, come get it!** My monster dick is thinking about me. That is what I am talking about. We are not together, but he thought enough to be thinking about me even though he is with someone else.

At least I am on his mind. Makes me wonder if Goldie ass is even with his woman, since he was calling me as well. It must be think of "INDIGO" night. Hell! I am not mad at any of them. I know how to put it down, and make a man call for his momma. They probably fucking some timid ass woman, scared to fuck with the lights on and shit. Just thinking about... **BEEP...** Smiling and checking my text knowing it's him again. **Send me a pic of that pussy!** Scooting down to the edge of the sofa; pulling my boy shorts to the side, and raising my left leg up until my foot is behind my head. Pussy gapping open; showing the pink sweet middle, pulling back the hood, so I can capture the prettiest protruding clit he has ever seen.

Snapping three shots in a row, the last one was with my two fingers deep inside of my pussy. Normally that would have made me want to masturbate, and cum a couple of times. But as fucking horny as I stay, I would rather have the touch of a man and the flesh of a real dick. No plastic dicks for me, unless it is used in addition to giving me double penetration. Shit! Nothing like a man who knows how to fuck you in different positions and have you walking bo-legged. The weekend is coming up. I think I need to put monster dick on the books. I need to get this pussy

beat up. Shit! I am so horny. Sending those pics to

his ass got my pussy dripping. Guess it's gonna be

a three finger night for me.

NO APOLOGIES

Derwin 11

This shit don't make no damn sense. This girl is crazy as fuck, but hell! Guess I am too. I don't give two fucks. I don't fuck over my damn feelings. Most niggas will call it a bitch move, on what I am about to do, but fuck that! I was making plans, and falling deeper in love with her. All she was able to do, was tell that she was in love with his ass. Like fuck me and my feelings. She don't know it, but damn it! She gonna pay for that shit. I walked away like a dog with his puppy tail tucked between his damn legs and this shit is not acceptable. I wanted to slap the fuck out of her when she told me that she was still in love with his no nothing ass.

NO APOLOGIES

Hell! He has even drove Chanta' ass crazy, and all she did was suck his dick. No relationship, no nothing and she done went off the deep end over his ass. I don't know what the fuck he do to their asses, but damn it! He need to take his trying to get legit ass on some fucking where. Shit! If any of my boys heard me talking like this, I would surely be a bitch ass nigga in their eyes. Their asses are use to fucking any bitch with two legs. They don't know shit about love, and what it is capable of doing to you when you are in it. Jasmine is the kind of woman, that makes a man want to give her any and everything she desires, or hell! Just even ask for.

NO APOLOGIES

That would have not been a problem for me at all. I am damn successful, and we could have took the world by storm; with her writing career being outstanding and me owning my damn business. My home is paid for, and I have no damn kids. I guess when people say that a woman rather have a no nothing ass nigga, other than a good man is true. I thought the damn woman had more sense than that shit. She's building shit on the fact that they are longtime friends and they have history. I needed more time to get her like I really wanted to, but her heart was on his ass. I swear she should have just told me that shit before I even fucked her; over and over, and over again.

NO APOLOGIES

Some shit I can deal with, but a pretty bitch who think that they can treat me however they want, and I am just suppose to take it, Will never do. I need to get in contact with Chanta', had to send her crazy ass home for a while. She was driving me insane. I have been at the dealership all day, and Wednesdays are usually slow. The weather is pretty mild for it to be mid September. All I really want to do is leave, grab me a beer and chill for the rest of the damn day. Or better yet, I think I may drive pass the new house Jasmine and that nigga living in and shit, like her living in the far suburbs is going to keep her out of my fucking grasp.

NO APOLOGIES

Yeah, I think that is a better deal other than go home and have a beer. Guess I will roll through her neighborhood in a black on black 1969 Mach 1 Mustang Fastback. My love for older model mustangs, has always had my attention. Ever since I was a kid. My father taught me that having the original is better than anything that they are remaking on the market today. Older model cars was built for speed and looks, and the body is phenomenal. While all my friends got the new 2014 stuff out, I will always role around in an old mustang. It's what I love. In fact, I call my mustang... Jasmine.

NO APOLOGIES

"Gary, lock up tonight. It is slow as fuck and I got shit to do. I will catch you later, maybe the weekend." Gary is a cool cat. Got down on his luck, and needed a job in the worst way. My dad always told me "never turn a person away based on their past" everyone has one. "Let their actions now speak for them" and that's what I did. When he came to me a year ago, he had no experience in the car business, but I taught him what he needed to know, to be successful. I wouldn't trade him for no one in the world, he is hard working and dependable.

He is a young twenty-six, but he let the drug game suck him in like so many of our youth. He made up his mind, that he was tired of going to jail, and sick and tired of the fucking police harassing him. I was proud to see him leave that street shit alone. "No problem boss, you know I will hold shit down here for you. Go do your thing, and I will see you when you pop back in." I was half way out the damn door before he even finished his damn sentence, but I heard enough. I knew he was saying his same line, every time I say I am gone for the day. Opening the car door to my baby, I knew I was looking good; high top black red bottoms, True Religion black jeans, with black shirt, displaying a TR in the upper left part of the shirt. Smelling good like a motherfucker; Ferragamo Cologne. Shit! It is a panty wetter for sure. Revering up the engine, and screeching away from the curb; letting Drake bounce around the inside of the car, heading in the direction of her new home, with this clown ass nigga shit looking around the suburban neighborhood. She has always done well for herself and this is no different. Shit! Thank goodness Chanta' had the address, so I can find this place. Thank goodness for the GPS. Hitting the block that she now resides on, rolling slowly until I hear the GPS say "I have made it to my destination on the right". Wow! Baby girl live in the big house now; big ass yard, big ass front porch. Shit! I see red and yellow balls on the lawn, two big large window panes on the left and right side of the main door.

NO APOLOGIES

Looks like I saw someone walk across the room and the only woman in the house, or should be in the house is my baby Jasmine. Shit! If they don't want no one peeking through their damn windows, they gonna need some curtains. Cause I am watching her go back and forth with a little child. Wow! She looks amazing. She wearing what appears to be a yellow sun dress, and her hair pulled back. Damn! Her ass is sitting up just right. Damn! She picking up that baby as if she gave birth to it her damn self. Bouncing her on her hip, looking dead at my car. Good thing my windows are tinted. She can't see a damn thing, but I can see all of her.

NO APOLOGIES

Walking away from the window, I see the front door open slowly; just watching me as I watch her, dick jumped hard as fuck, as soon as I saw her fucking face. I swear, I want to just jump the fuck out, and grab her tight as fuck. Damn! I am in love with her ass. She starting to look nervous. That's when I roll slowly pass her house, watching her in my rearview going back in the house. Damn! I am super charged right now. Shit! I want to call her now, but I know she probably will hang up. Since she's trying to do right in her relationship, but somehow I think she may change her mind. At some point Goldie is gonna fuck up, and when he does, I will be here to wipe away her tears, and give her this dick. Shit! She already have my damn

heart, and that I wish she would give back.

NO APOLOGIES

Chanta' 12

Out of all the fucking we been doing, I knew that motherfucker would be down for anything I suggest when it comes to fucking up Jasmine and Goldie little happy home. That should teach them about playing with people's feelings. It's just some shit you just don't do and it's about time they understood that they don't walk on water. In fact, their shit do stank. I knew Goldie wasn't shit. With all the shit I've seen him put Jasmine through, I should have known, but hell her ass was in NYC. Shit! I knew with a little time, I could have had him. Shit! For goodness sake, he is only a man.

NO APOLOGIES

I didn't get a chance to sleep with him, but the moment his dick was in my mouth, I knew we was on to a great start. But oh no, Ms. Thang had to show her ass back up here and go after the one man, she said over and over again that she didn't want. I guess you never want someone until you see them moving on, or someone else is interested in them. I know she looks at me like a fool of a friend, but hey his ass was on the market and shit. He came for me, just as much as I came for him, but she don't see that. He get a pass, but I don't?

Ain't that bout a bitch! I guess you gotta be fucking a nigga to get a pass. What the hell ever! I have heard her ass on so many fucking occasions, she says she don't give a fuck, or she have a side dip here or there. I bet Goldie would love to know that about his sweet, precious little Jasmine. It's this one guy she has went on and on about for years. I thought she was going to end up with his ass, as loose as she was in the ass. I'm sure while Goldie was eating her pussy, he tasted cum that was left from the side dude on more than one occasion.

Yup, I don't even have to touch her or him, to fuck up both of their worlds. I think I will spill the beans on little Ms. Jasmine, and see what happens. I can almost guarantee, that I will be fucking Goldie before it is all over with. That of course will fuck

Jasmine head up. Which will add fuel to the fire. I admit, I can be a dirty bitch. I mean hey; when I want to make a person pay, I find ways to make that shit happen. They are no different from anyone else that fuck with me. Walking around my apartment barefooted is great, but I rather be with Derwin right now.

I have been getting on his damn nerves I see and someone was on the verge of getting cussed the fuck out. I be damned if it was gonna be me, so it was best that I leave. I will see him this coming weekend. Of course, we will be doing some much needed fucking. He hooked on Jasmine and I am hooked on Goldie, yet we fucking each other. I refuse to continue fucking someone who is in love with another woman. I wouldn't say that I am deeply in love with Goldie, but the more I think about this; it is more revenge for having his dick in my mouth, and trying to treat me like he does the rest of his hoes.

I know my information I got on Jasmine is going to crush his ass and that is pleasure enough for me. Now Jasmine on the other hand, she has always thought she was better than everyone else she has come across. You couldn't and can't tell her ass shit. I guess if you hear all your life how fine you are you start to believe it.

NO APOLOGIES

No work for me today at the department store, so it will be a wine day for me. I am only going to rest and relax my ass off. Hell! If I was smarter, I should not have gotten so caught up in him and laid low; played my role and maybe I would be living in a bigger place. Other than this one bedroom I am currently in.

My life is falling apart. I don't give shit about my damn job. I am fucking a man who is in love with another woman, I want to fuck a man who is in love with another woman, and I want to fuck up my ex-best-friend's relationship. Yeah this shit screams "Iyanla fix my life" If Derwin would just get her out of his mind, then maybe we could try and be together with no Goldie and no Jasmine in our lives. I think he is more hell bent on making her pay, then I am on making Goldie pay.

I just brought that "fuck up their life" shit to see what he would say. He looked liked he needs to get some shit off his chest. No matter how much I fuck and suck him, he still can't get that chick out of his system.

Damn! just sitting here watching old re-runs of Girlfriends, really got me to thinking about a lot of shit and this shit is getting more and more depressing my the second. I should call Goldie ass right now and see if he wants to hear what I have to say, or maybe I should hold on to this little bit of information, until I see what Derwin has planned for this plan of ours. Looks like these sorry bitches got just as many men problems on this television program, as we do in the real world. Shit! When a woman is falling for a man, she will jump through hoops to try and keep his ass. When that motherfucker ain't trying to give a woman no act right, then well, she just gonna have to teach his ass a lesson. Niggas jump from women like they are changing their fucking clothes.

Damn! This wine is good and it's putting me in the mood to start some shit. I am ready to jump start this bullshit ass game of action, so I can get it over with. I need this and I need to start it now. A motherfucker can call it whatever they like, but just seeing the pure hurt on his face will be priceless to me. Fuck it! I am going to start my shit today. I can't wait on Derwin ass. Searching my couch cushions for my damn phone; finally pulling it out yes indeed, his ass is about to hear from me today. And I am not sending no damn text either. **Ring… Ring… Ring…** After the third ring he finally picks up, his ass makes me sick at times.

"What up doe," he answers. "Hey Goldie how are you?" I say. "Who dis?" He responds. "Chanta'." "WHO?" I take the phone away from my ear, and let out a deep breath, this dude can't be serious. "Chanta'! Don't play Goldie like you don't know who this is." "Chanta' I didn't know this was you, your number was not saved in my phone, but since you calling what's up?" "I was wondering if we could meet up and talk." Damn! That was lame as hell, should have come better than that. "You know, I just don't get down and meet to have talks and shit. So you gonna have to say what the hell is on your mind now."

See I knew this asshole was going to show up but as soon as I utter those words 'Jasmine' then he will perk the hell up. "Damn! I just figured that we did have a nice little connection. I thought calling wouldn't be a problem." "Stop thinking so damn much Chanta', but when you can say whatever it is that made you call me then do so

until then have a good one." "Wait! Hold on

Goldie, I do have one word to say....JASMINE!"

NO APOLOGIES

Alexis 13

I don't know where the fuck he is right now and I don't give two shits. I'm the woman up in his damn house. I am the one he lays his head on when he is sleepy and I am the one he calls every hour, on the hour. Hell! I knew in the beginning he had other women that he may or may not sleep with, but hell! I have a couple folks I sleep with on the side as well. I have grown to love Curtis ass, and maybe one-day when we both are done playing, we can settle down and make it right between us. I have not been at my house as much as I should be. Most of the time I am here by my damn self, or he comes in so damn late from either working, or being out with one of his lady friends.

Frankly, I am tired of acting like I need to change in the other room and shit. I feel like in a way, I can't be who I really am around him. His shit is getting on my nerves. Like tonight, I am laying in this massive king bed by myself; letting the music of Jill Scott swoon through his condo. I am tired of masturbating. I am in need of a man who can hold me, and wants to keep me. But I signed on to this shit with Curtis, and there is no telling who he is with tonight. Got me laying in bed wearing nothing but a lace teddy; like I am waiting on him. Actually, this is the way I go to bed every night, but I would like to be here with him between my legs giving me the business.

Fuck that! Man got a monster dick on him, and then have the nerve to flip a sistah around too, just to eat my pussy. Man he can damn sho put it down on my ass. Hell! I am bored. I need to contact my bestie Jerome ass. I haven't heard from his ass in a few weeks. Wonder what the fuck he up to. Reaching in my black Dior purse I grabbed my phone to holla at his ass **Ring... Ring...**

"Aww hell no Ms. Thang, where the hell have you been, and what the hell you doing at this very moment?" "Well if you must know Jerome, I'm laying in bed with a teddy on at eleven at night waiting on my man to come home. Actually bored out of my fucking mind. I went into work today; did five heads and left up out of there." "Damn girl! You could have called me sooner. We could have went out and had some drinks or something." See I knew Jerome would understand. Hell! He about the only one who actually does understand what I am talking about, and I am truly thankful for his friendship.

"Why don't you come over here Jerome and we can have drinks here. I just don't really want to go out." "Now Ms. Thang, you know I am on my way to get into some shit. That's why I said you should have said something early." "I truly understand

NO APOLOGIES

Jerome, I am just feeling out of sorts." Fuck! What is wrong with me? I go from happy to sad in a matter of just a few moments, and I just can't figure this shit out. Laying in the middle of the bed, in a fetal position. It has got to get better than this shit. "I've told you many times why you feel the way you feel and until you be true with you, then you are always gonna feel unfulfilled. Don't be scared to be who you are Ms. Thang, fuck that! You know I love you boo."

"You are right Jerome. I must be true to myself and fuck the bullshit." Jerome always knows what's wrong with me no matter what and as always, he is right. I truly take his advice to heart. I guess I need do what I need to do, to make my life better for me; not for anyone else. "Hell, I am always right you know that! I just don't like to see you waiting for a man and not one hundred percent sure if he gonna stay when you start being the true you Alexis boo." "Ugh! This shit is driving me insane. I can't do shit but pray that this shit is going to work-out Jerome. I've just been trying to be the one everyone wants me to be, that's all."

I heard Jerome take a deep sigh over the phone before he spoke. "Ms. Thang, ummm... who the hell is everyone? They only see what you project. You need to put your representative away and introduce yourself. Cause you driving me insane!"

Hearing Jerome go in on me, in his Nawlins'

accent; it started showing the faster he talked. I

was on the verge of hanging up; he has this way of

making you feel bad and telling you the truth, all

at the same damn time. Jerome has never been

the one, as long as I have known him, to lie about

anything. All the shit that he has been through;

good, bad and the ugly.

 He always tell folks that are closes to him "no

need to start of lying, cause' that will be how you

end shit" is what he will always say. I just wish I

was just as brave as he is. "Ms.Thang, you need to

get out and go find you some dick to land on.

NO APOLOGIES

Trust! That shit will make you feel better. Oh! But wait, you falling in love and shit!" "Don't shit on my love for Charles. Hell! If you try it, maybe you will like it!" "No you didn't Ms. Thang! I know love. I love you and you only. That's all the love I need right now." "Now, you just trying to get on my good side Jerome." "No, just speaking facts and if and when the time comes, when I want to live in love, I will let it find me. Until then, I am partying and having a ball, which is what you should be doing your damn self."

"Yeah I know, but this is where I want to be right now. I am just glad that I have you to talk to no matter what. I love you boo." "Keep your I love you boo, u know, love you too. I'm in these streets, so I'll get in contact with you later in the week. Take a kiss for you, bye boo." "Bye boo." After the phone clicked off, I was sure that my life was about to change. Just didn't know when and where I was going to be, when it does. Frankly, I am getting tired of this; he out and I'm in the house, in this bed alone.

Even though I came into this knowing that we would do us; we both are free to do other people. That's been a little over a year and damn! I don't need to fuck no other dude other than him. It's time we have a talk after he stroll his ass in here. I know he not gonna want to hear shit I have to say,

NO APOLOGIES

but damn it! it's time. If things are not gonna go

any further than this, then I am going to have to

leave after a while. All this fucking random people

is for the birds.

You have met folks, got the

back story on folks and now it's

time to shake some shit up!

But I must warn you this is

what the characters wanted

they have a mind of their own I

am just writing THEIR story!

NO APOLOGIES

Alexis 14

Swerving through this bullshit ass traffic in the rain so I don't be late for my damn hair appointment with Jerome, has put me in a bad a mood. The fact that Curtis ass is still hanging out more and more these days, he says it's his job. He putting down some great beats for up and coming rap stars, that's doing a lot of underground work right now. He throws little hints out there; letting me know when he about to be knee deep in some pussy. Like saying "I don't know what time I will be home, late nights early morning" shit like that. To let me know he on some other pussy that particular night.

NO APOLOGIES

Finally getting to Jerome's shop, I can only hope he's ready now and not in here on some flamboyant shit today. I need him ready; ready to work. To my surprise, I see the same damn red car as before. I can't remember her name, but I know she was getting on my damn nerves. Stepping out the car with my umbrella over my head; trying to run in and not get drenched as much as I already was. As soon as the chimes over the door clanged together, four pair of eyes was looking back at me.

"Heyyyy Ms. Thang, I see you finally made it out here in all this damn rain and shit. I just knew your ass was gonna cancel on me." Shaking out my umbrella at the door, before walking towards him and giving him an air kiss, I acknowledge the person sitting in the chair getting a sharp ass edgy cut. Which means this is the one who drives the red car. "Heyyy girl! I see you are getting that damn hair laid. Shit! That style is sharp as hell. I might have to get mines cut like that. I'm feeling that."

"Thanks boo, you know Jerome. He may get on your damn nerves, but he knows how to do some hair. I don't trust anyone to do it, that's why I keep bringing my too cute ass down here in the hood." Jerome smacked his damn lips. It almost echoed throughout the salon. Whenever he does that, it's his way of saying excuse the fuck out of me, or you got your damn nerve. "Just have a seat in the other chair Ms. Thang. I will be with you shortly, and I don't appreciate y'all laughing it up at my expense. "

   "Jerome you know we love you, but as long as you got them damn scissors in my hair, I won't be saying much of anything else. I don't shut up for no one, but when it comes to my hair, I won't be saying another word at least until you finish." All three of us started laughing and talking about all sorts of shit in general. I found out that Indigo is cool as hell. She can rub you the wrong way most of the time. She kind of lives her life, the way most of us do; make the best out of a bad situation. She saw that her assets could let her live a comfortable life, and she capitalized on it.

When the topic of sex and threesomes came up, the room was live. We learned that Jerome been fucking boy/men since he was fourteen, doing whatever he had to do to stay off Nawlins' streets. Sometimes that meant sleeping with men. Jerome said he has always known he was gay but he didn't have his parents around. His mom didn't know who his daddy was and his mom was battling her own street demons. Hearing Indigo talk about all her sexcapades with all these different men, was not a shock but made me feel like I was missing out on life. Just living it the way I want to.

She had mentioned that she was head over heels with some guy named Goldie, but he has since then went back to his girlfriend. The whole story sounded crazy from beginning to end but Jerome and I listened to every word. Now she on this new kick, with a new dick that she calls "monster dick." She never said his name but I see she was really fond of him. Then when I told my story, of how Jerome and I met in Nawlins' when I was on vacation and how we just hit it off. Indigo learned that I was also gay; now turned transgender, born Alex, now Alexis. I couldn't be happier telling them that the guy I'm seeing has no clue that I was ever a guy. Makes for a damn good reality show. Indigo grew some concerns when I said he doesn't know it, seemed genuine enough for me to explain.

"Excuse me for being so forward; How can he not know he fucking a transgender. I mean when he eating you and fucking you, he can't tell that you wasn't born a woman and this is just random; why do you and Charles wear matching bracelets?" Damn she is blunt. "Well if you must know. We always have sex in the dark or by candle light. If we shower together, I always make sure my back is turned to him, and when I change and lotion up my body, I go in the spare bedroom so I don't have to keep turning in different angles.

The funny thing about it is, he just thinks I just have an enormous clit. Now about the bracelets, the life we live is not accepted by everyone. Neither one of us have anyone close in our lives that we would consider family but each other. It's like our own life alert bracelets; should anything ever happen to us, then they would know who to call." Whatever Indigo was drinking, came flying across the room when I mentioned enormous clit, she fell out laughing. I leaned to the left in the chair, so her drink wouldn't get on me. Jerome and I laughed too. I guess my little secret is not that bad after all.

 "Look Alexis, I know I just really met you, the last time we didn't hit if off too well, but what I do know; good, bad or otherwise, people are gonna have something to say about you, so you may as well live how you want. If he still want you after you tell him fine, if he don't, then leave his ass standing with his dick in his hand." Wow, I didn't expect for her to give me that kind of advice. She can come off as a person who don't give to fucks about no one but herself and she's saying the same damn thing that Charles has been saying for the longest time.

NO APOLOGIES

See Ms.Thang, I told you right. While you sitting around here worried about what he gonna say or anyone for that matter. I say fuck them, fuck them all! What they eat don't make you shit, so you really shouldn't have a fucking care in the world."

"Look Alexis, if me and Jerome saying the same thing to you, then it's time you listen to someone. This life is short and it don't make no sense to live it unhappily or not to your full potential. "

Sitting back in my chair, listening to them run their mouth on 'why do I need to tell this secret' and tell it now. I didn't want to tell him so soon. I've still been waiting for the right time to say something. No one wants to hear they have been

NO APOLOGIES

fucking a transgender. I know he has feelings for me and I have feelings for him. I live as a woman. I am a woman; I really fully want to be his woman, and I guess there is no time like the present to tell him this lie that has went on long enough.

NO APOLOGIES

Goldie 15

Loving the way my damn Mentor Program is coming along, there are children that actually come here faithfully. I have truly made this a safe haven for them. If I can save one child, then this was very much worth it. I know I was a thug ass nigga in them streets and hell I battle that shit every day, so I know what it is like to wanna run the streets; make quick money and sleep with as many women as you want. Then you have them bitch niggas out there on those streets, not giving a fuck about no one and nothing. Just whatever it is they want. They don't mind grabbing little boys and girls and making them do all kinds of fucked up shit for an audience. That's just as fucked up as they are.

I would have given my right arm, and took a bullet to get this program up and running and to see it thriving the way that it is; lets me know that I have done something right. I got a couple of the teenagers helping around here; cleaning and doing light stuff. Of course I pay them handsomely. I don't ever want to look a child in the face that's telling me that they want to hit the streets for more money. This is truly a dream come true for me. Not everyone shares in my happiness, but that's okay. I have one person who

NO APOLOGIES

I know believes in me, even though she living foul as fuck right now.

It's been a few weeks since I even brought up the fact that she trying to do playa shit with a fucking a fucking playa. She must don't know no damn better. I been playing bitches for a long ass time. It ain't one thing out here that I haven't done, when it comes to faking and fucking. Now unless she's been watching me over the years, she may have picked up some pointers. Still you can't fuck over me; all you can do is keep getting dicked by me and whomever else is willing to fuck you. Hope I don't let you hang your damn self. I know I ain't shit and I knew she was gonna eventually do some foul shit, but if she don't start making this shit clean, then I am gonna have to pull her hoe card real quick.

Making sure the program is running smoothly, I make sure the books are looking real good; the bills are paid. I found real good potential in rehabbing run down, old houses and reselling them for a great fucking profit. Jasmine and I work on that together. It keeps us busy and we find the shit dirt cheap; always turning a profit, always pushing forward. I can't believe she decided for shit to be going good between us, to pull this bullshit. Leaving the mentor program; headed downtown to see some new places, I haven't been looking into condos, but what can I say? Money is money, and as long as the return is long, I am in.

Meeting Ms. Pearson at the high rise of condos, I was excited. Valeted my car and walked into the building as she waited for me in the lobby. Walking in as cool as I am; dreads coiled, no cap on today, Gucci shades, Gucci sweater, black jeans, and a pair of black Gucci casual high tops, with the Gucci sign on the side. Ms. Pearson had a voluptuous Jill Scott thing going on from her smile, to her form fitting clothes. Damn! She older I know, but I may have to tap that shit! Extending my hand out to hers, we gave a firm hand shake; all business and no personal.

NO APOLOGIES

"Thanks for meeting me on such short notice Mr. Miller. I saw that this property opened up just a week ago and I came straight to you with it. I know you haven't done anything with condos before but I think this is a beautiful choice in property. So if you don't mind, follow me to the seventeenth floor where we can go see your new baby." She lead the way and my goodness did she lead; ass was mesmerizing, hips was gratifying just by looking and all I can envision is her legs wrapped around my head, using her thighs as ear muffs.

I have seen her many times before but we always kept it casual and business, but damn!

NO APOLOGIES

That black dress she wearing is on point. Riding the elevator up to the seventeenth floor, she continues on how great the property is. How I got for a real great price; it is a really good investment. Looking at how great she looked, I started hearing Charlie Brown teacher, until the elevator doors chimed and opened for us. As we were getting off the elevator, a man was getting on. He was a well-built man, dressed well, hell! He even smelled good. She almost lit up when she saw him, but tried to contain herself.

"Oh Mr. Miller, this is Mr. Walker. He resides here as well and he believes it to be a fabulous place to call home." Ms. Pearson was all smiles;

touching him every time she said any word, oh yeah, she got a thing for this dude, but I will change that shit. "Hey Bro, I am in a hurry, but if you are looking to invest in this property, it is awesome! I wouldn't change a thing about it. And to you Ms. Pearson as always it is a pleasure to see you." We hopped out, he hopped in and we were headed to condo 1715. The halls was nice; decorated with pictures of black art, a saxophone player, woman and man embraced, all sorts of amazing art. I kinda like this shit. She opened the door and walked in. I was instantly hit with the smell of fresh paint, not over bearing but you can tell it was painted.

NO APOLOGIES

"I am so sorry about the smell Mr. Miller the workers must have done this last night I truly apologize." She was running around cutting on ceiling fans, and fanning herself with her folder, and being very apologetic. When in fact, I really don't care about the smell. I couldn't get my eyes off of her long enough to think about anything else. Walking closer to her, I can smell the sweet smell she has planted on her neck and my dick is ready to taste something else. "Calm down sweetie, I am fine. The smell is not bothering me but I will tell you what is bothering me."

As I talked, she walks to the windows that is from corner to corner in the room, getting me to see that I can see downtown city lights. As if I really care for that shit but this ass that is staring back at me, got me ready to fuck now. "So Mr. Miller, you can take your time and look around. If you have any questions, let me know." She smiled a come fuck me smile, and that's a smile I recognize anywhere. "Yes I have one question, if I ate your pussy now, would you let me fuck you too?" The look on her face was fucking priceless. I meant what I asked, and she was not ready for that, but her body language has gotten looser. I think I am about to sink this one right about now. Her body language has given it away.

NO APOLOGIES

"Ummm don't you have a girlfriend Mr. Miller?"

"First off yes, and second please, just call me

Goldie." "Well Goldie, since you have a girl, what

you need me for?" Oh shit, here we go; watching

her cross her arms over her chest, let me know

she got to be taken down a peg. I do a half smile,

and chuckle barely above a whisper, just to see

her reaction to my every move; rubbing my index

finger along the outline of her beautiful face. "I

am sorry to inform you Tamia, but I don't need

you; I want you, there is a big difference."

"Hmmm is that so?" That's so just like a woman,

to think all men need their asses.

NO APOLOGIES

Next thing I heard was all the papers hit the floor and her breast hitting my chest. She wanted to see what damage I could do and I damn show plan to have her ass limping away. She began to walk backwards slowly, unraveling her belt that's attached to her dress. Once her dress hit the floor nothing but a lace black bra and panty was exposed. "If you want this pussy come, get this pussy." Damn! Hearing her say those words got me harder than I was before. I'm about to go to town on her ass. "Baby, you see the windowsill, go stand in front of that and drop them panties for me."

NO APOLOGIES

Seeing her wiggle out of her panties, and bend over; her pussy was already wet, it was even calling my damn name. "That's it baby. I'm going to eat your pussy from the back. I want you to let all those juices flow in my mouth." "Mmmm whatever you want baby, I've been dreaming about this day for a long ass time. Finally I get to have you." Bending down, until my knees hit the floor, I hike her ass up some, so I can get at her pussy just a little bit better. Slowly licking and inhaling the sweet smell of new pussy. I continue to lick and rub on her ass; tongue fucking her, licking up and down her walls, sucking soft and hard on her swelling clit.

NO APOLOGIES

She starts to grind her pussy on my face, rotating her hips left, right, then in circles. Damn! This woman taste sweet as hell. Damn! I'm glad I made the move to taste her. Alternating between tongue fucking her and sucking on her clit, I hear her moans getting louder and louder. "Oh shit! Goldie baby, yes, right there. I am about to cum all in your mouth." "That's it baby, give me them sweet ass juices, fuck you taste so damn good." My sounds are muffled, but can be heard. I continued to grind and I continued to eat until I felt her body get stiff as a board, then relaxed, while she like to drowned the fuck out of me.

NO APOLOGIES

While she squirted all over me, her cries could be heard in the hallway. The tangy, yet sweet taste of her ran down the sides of my mouth; dripping off my chin and landing on my sweater. I continued to tease her clit while I stood up. She started twirling her hips and playing with her pussy. Keeping her hot for me as I unfasten my pants and pulled the rock out. I slide up close on her and rubbed the head up against her soaked pussy. Easy as pie, I slide in and once I hear that "GASP" I know she done for.

I didn't wait to find a groove. My mode was set on high so that is exactly what the fuck I did, I drilled her ass like I was looking for oil. Grabbing her around her hips, diving in deep with long forceful thrusts over and over again. I speed up, I feel my nut building, fuck she gripping my dick like an ant caught in honey. The tighter she gripped me, the faster I fucked her. I pulled her back, so she can grab her ankles; head down-ass up, my hands pressed down on the small her back, pumping into her for dear life. "Oh shit Baby! I am about to cum, let daddy see you swallow my cum baby."

She turned around and swooped my dick in her mouth, giving me nothing but neck action, grabbing her hair and forcing her down on my dick as I erupted in her throat. She gagged so much, it started oozing out the sides of her mouth where it

began running down her neck, and chin. Damn!

The sight of her sucking everything I had in me,

could have made me faint on that alone.

Stumbling some, as I re-tract my dick from her

mouth, watching her wipe her mouth with the

back of her hand, her hair is disheveled and she

has the look of drunken sex on her face. Helping

her to her feet, watching her as she searched for

her clothes and ran to the bathroom to fix her

hair. Fuck! I did this shit again, but this time I got a

damn good reason to.

"Goldie babe, you laid some serious dick on me.

I totally was not expecting it but glad it

happened." Looking at her, she was stumbling as she put her heels back on. She put her panties in her purse while trying to pick up her papers that she had thrown to the floor once she knew, she was about to get some of this dick. "I understand you was trying to be professional and what not but what I want, I get."

Standing against the opposite wall from her, I spoke as I straightened out my clothes the best I knew how, her juices soaked through my shirt. Still smelling the sweet smell of her around my mouth; still feeling the tightening of her insides, hearing the orgasmic sounds she was making, feeling her wetness as it travels through her, onto me. I still feel the rounds of her ass in the palms of my hands, and the dip of her lower back imprinted on my finger tips.

This woman has tattooed herself within me. "Look, as you know, I am going to buy this place, and who knows, I may just keep it, instead of selling it. You never know who wants to come over." Raising my eyebrow in her direction, giving her a hint that he was already expecting her to come his way. I love thick thigh women with big assess. That shit turns me the fuck on. I think Tamia' will be a damn good fuck buddy, for a while anyway.

NO APOLOGIES

Indigo 16

"Curtis, when can you call me? I'm way over do for your deep dick action; it's been far too long." Pressing the end button on my phone, feeling pissed, throwing the phone face down on my bed, I don't know what the fuck is up. I looked on my calendar, I've been through two periods and haven't seen his ass. I don't know what or who he has fell up in, but I know it's some other woman's pussy. The streets and pussy are the only two things that will keep a man from coming around like he should. I don't mind that he fucking around, hell! That's what men do, but I don't like the fact that he is trying to be slick about it.

NO APOLOGIES

He knows we don't have any secrets. No real

secrets at least but if he thinks he is gonna have

me sitting around like I don't have shit to do, he is

sadly mistaken. Hell, shit like this make me wanna

call up Goldie ass and see what the fuck he up to.

Shit, if he can call me out the blue, I damn sho can

call him out the blue as well. **Ring... Ring... Ring...**

You know who you called, leave me a

message...one

Hey Goldie, this is Indigo. Hit me up, I haven't

seen you in a while. Ain't that some shit, he sent

me to voicemail. What the fuck he doing so damn

important? Okay, I see all these niggas on some

bullshit and they must forgot who the fuck I am. I don't bullshit y'all, so don't bullshit me.

Hmmm, look at this shit, now my phone wanna ring back. I shouldn't even answer cause I'm sure it is one of these men. "Hello?" "Hey Ms. Pretty pussy." "Curtis, where have you been? And please just give me the quick version." See here come some ol' bullshit. I don't want to hear nothing about him being in the studio all night making beats and what not. I want to hear the truth, nothing more; nothing less. I don't have time for this. "Well, I will say we need to talk, and I don't want to discuss this shit over the phone, so how about I come over your house later on tonight?"

NO APOLOGIES

If this nigga think he's coming over my damn house to fuck, he out of his rabbit ass mind. Talking is all we gonna do and I am not in the mood for no lying dick. It always amazes me when you give a nigga the green light and be honest. He still finds ways to lie to you and it is always some bullshit. Hell! I know I got some bomb ass pussy and my head game will have a nigga's soul leave their body, so why he fucking someone else is beyond me.

Today will be a shop therapy day for me. I haven't been shopping in a while and I truly need some therapy. These niggas gonna drive me crazy if I let them. It's fucked up how I have burned so many bridges, I may have to go shopping by my damn self. Maybe my good associate Belynda, wanna hang with me? Hell, even she be acting funny at times. I'll just send her a damn text, just in case she don't want to go. I don't want her to have to beat around the bush until she gets to the one that says "NO."

Hey girl it's been a minute since we last hung out, wanna go do some shopping? Hit me back. She only getting thirty minutes tops or I'm going to have to leave. I don't wait on no one. It's either you do or you don't want to hang with me. **Beep, Beep...** Damn that was quick. I didn't expect her to text back so damn fast. Looking at my phone and realized that it was Goldie ass. **Hey, I was busy earlier what's up?** This nigga and his smug ass attitude. I've had just about enough of this shit. If Jasmine loves it, good for her. This shit is old and I don't want to have to deal with it anymore.

I don't want nothing, don't worry about it. This will be my last damn text. I don't deal with bullshit. He try and treat people like he the king, everyone else is peasants. Fuck that!! A big dick is not worth all the stress, but damn if his dick ain't big! An hour later; I showered, changed into some fitted blue jeans, black heels and a fitted gray sweater. Hair pulled back into a tight bun and my two carat diamond studs in each ear. Checking out my look in the full length mirror, shit! I know

I'm the shit. This outfit with this ass is a winner.

Grabbing my Gucci jacket out the hall closet,

dimming my lights and grabbing my keys out of

my purse, I was ready to go. It was only five in the

evening; plenty time left in the day to do what I

wanted to do.

NO APOLOGIES

Curtis 17

"I am glad you asked me to come get you. I am surprised that you just didn't take a cab. Trust and believe, I don't mind coming to get you from anywhere." Jazzi and I walked into my condo; watching her tight ass sway from side to side, I didn't know how much I missed her, until I had her turned upside down and her pussy was in my mouth. I know we don't have much time to play. Her man has got her on lock down, but I do plan to eat something today. Jazzi kicked off her shoes as she walked; slipping, twisting and turning out of her jeans, exposing a red lace thong with a butterfly at the top of it. Her breast was imprisoned buy a matching red lace bra. Twenty feet from the door, she hopped on the counter, spread her legs and commanded I come to her.

Leaving my clothes in the middle of the floor, I knew it was time to dive in. She wanted her pussy eaten just as bad as I wanted to eat it. Walking up to her, sniffing out her scent before I was even close enough to actually smell it. The scent of sweet hot pussy is invading my nose a little at a time, until I get so damn close, it wraps around my throat through my nostrils and into my mouth. Salivating; tasting her scent, needing her, wanting her so bad, I am in love with her and she don't even know it.

NO APOLOGIES

"That's it baby, come to me, smell this pussy, taste this pussy." Touching every inch of her body as if I need to get reacquainted every time I am with her, is new to me all over again. Standing in between her legs, rubbing her legs softly from her ankles up to her thighs, caressing her inner thighs; we keep an intoxicating stare on each other. Thumbing her pussy through her panties with one hand as I guide my hand up to her breast. Gliding my hand over each harden nipple. This woman is so mesmerizing to me, it could rain forever and I would still be dry under the umbrella of Jasmine.

Knowing her for over ten years, making the many trips I have taken to NYC to see her, makes this all worthwhile. No matter how much she say she love that other nigga, I know damn well she loves me too. "That pussy wet for me Jazzi? That's what I like," softly speaking with every word I speak. She bit down on her bottom lip and seductively licked her lips. Leaning in to kiss each breast, pulling her nipples out from the bra that is holding them captive, with every lick or flick of my tongue, her body shivers; trembles.

She is ready to explode, her body only gets like that when she ready to cum. Kissing down her stomach; rubbing every inch of her curved body, sliding her panties to the side, to expose a bare pussy, with a phat clit that is ready for licking.

NO APOLOGIES

Spreading her lips, licking up and down each side.

In and out, sucking on her clit and then humming

on it, repeat and do it again. Her body is writhing

under my touch. I scoop my hands under her ass

and hold her tight. I want to get every drop she is

about to explode in my mouth. Her beautiful

sounds where bouncing of the walls, the floor,

and off of me. Her legs were wrapped around my

head. I wanted to see that pussy cream. Opening

her legs further and pushing them back, sucking

on her clit long and strong. While inserting two

fingers in her ass for an orgasmic explosion.

"OH FUCK! CURTIS EAT THIS PUSSY, AND FINGER

FUCK THIS ASS. THIS IS YOUR PUSSY BABY. DON'T

NO APOLOGIES

STOP! DON'T STOP! I AM ABOUT TO CREAM ALL IN YOUR MOOOUUTTHH!" "That's it baby, that's it. This pussy so fucking good. I could eat you all fucking day, this my pussy? Say that shit again." "This your pussy baby." "Jasmine I love you, Jasmine I love you, Jasmine I love..." "You know I love you too, I been hiding you for way too long." Trying to pull her soul out with every drop that I catch in my mouth; this pussy juice should be packaged and sold on the market.

"Fuck me baby! I need this dick and I need this dick now." Letting my dick find its way to the of opening of heaven; dipping the head in and out, watching her chest move up and down, faster and faster, every time I dipped my dick in her tight pussy. Twirling her nipple between my fingers, until I reach her neck and applying some force like she like it. Building speed; watching her breast giggle when I thrust into her, harder, harder trying to give her my love through penetrating her Paradise.

"Fuck Jazzi! This pussy is the fucking best, it's the fucking best, I'm right here babe, I'm right here. I'm not going anywhere, I want you Jazzi!" "Right there Curtis baby, you hitting my fucking spot. That's, that's it, that's it. You are making this pussy leak all over the place." She moaning loud, I am moaning loud, it doesn't get any better than fucking the one you love. I could live in this pussy.

This fucking girl has had my heart from the very

beginning and I know damn well if she just got up

off old boy, she would gladly be with me.

Increasing speed; feeling my nut traveling from

my balls and ready to explode all over her,

pumping harder, squeezing her neck, sweat

dripping off my nose onto her stomach. "It's

cumin Jazzi, It's…CUMMIINN!" I pullout and jack

my dick all over her pussy and stomach. My knees

are about to buckle, I always have a strong nut

with her. That shit make me dizzy as fuck.

Collapsing on her as her body continue to shake as

our cum marry. "Let me taste us baby."

NO APOLOGIES

Tasting her again, as I dipped my tongue inside her; collect our juices, bringing it back to her lips, watching mouth open slightly, and she grab hold of my tongue, sucking on it for dear life. Enjoying our time together as always. The fucking best feeling is to have her near me. It's the best thing in the world. I just hope she realize that she fucking with a real man and not that shit of a man she loving on.

****

Full of emotions after Jasmine left nine at night on a Friday, not much to do except hit the club, or stay in. I'd rather stay in. I even packed Alexis clothes. I'm at this point: tired of the bullshit, the back and forth. She fucking other people and so am I, so I don't want to play this fucking game any longer. I have been fucking two women who are great to fuck, but that's it, that's all. I am tired of seeing Jasmine ass on the side, it's time I make her mines. This is going to be a chill night for me. Patron' on the rocks and watch me some basketball. I feel like I just want to chill in my own damn house, sip a little something and get my shit together. Hell, I don't even want to see Indigo.

I know I said we needed to talk face to face but damn it, I don't feel like no bullshit. All she is going to get from me is a fucking phone call.

NO APOLOGIES

Ring… Ring… Ring…. "Hello." "Hey Ms. Indigo."

"Ms. Indigo, I haven't heard that in a long while."

Here we go. "I hear a lot of movement in the back

ground, you need me to call you back?" "No, not

at all. I was just coming in the house with bags

and kicking off heels and what not."

"Well, I want to talk to you. I didn't want to talk

on the phone but I decided that I didn't want to

come back out. I just got to get this shit off my

chest, so here goes…I am ending our

relationship." I was all set to hear her go off and

tell me I ain't shit but she took another approach

that I didn't even see coming. "Wow you must

landed in some diamond ass pussy for you to want

to give this all up. You are one of the biggest fools I have come across in along ass time. Let me ask you a quick question is one of the chicks you fucking name Alexis?"

How the fuck she know anything about who I'm fucking? I don't talk to her ass about nothing, not even my business shit. Where the fuck she trying to go with this shit? "In fact it is. What of it?" "Well Mr. Smartass, since you done fucked up and left all this good ass pussy that you will never be able to sniff, taste, or go deep in again. It is my pleasure to let you know that I have ran into her a few times, we get our hair done at the same fucking place. Seems like we was fucking the same dude. What you didn't know is, the bitch you are currently fucking use to me a man...bloop!"

With those words ringing in my damn ears I heard the phone click off and I was in utter shock. Nawl, this shit can't be right. I stood up, start pacing, knocking shit on the floor. The mere thought of having my dick anywhere near a fucking man, is ringing death in my fucking ears. I'm literally gonna kill this bitch! I'm gonna KILL THIS BITCH!!!! Ranting and raving, look at who the fuck walks through the damn door. "Hey baby, damn it's ha...," the look on her face; wondering what just happened in the house, broken glass all on the floor, chairs that sat at my bar was across the room and she was staring a beast in the face.

"BITCH!"

Before I knew it, my hands was around her fucking neck, squeezing the fucking life out of her. She couldn't breathe, her eyes was rolling showing only the whites of her eyes. She started spitting, kicking, scratching me on my arms; trying her damn best to fuck me up but that shit wasn't happening. Fuck that! Slap... Slap... I must have slapped her ass from one end of the house to the other, about a hundred times. Then back to choking her ass almost to death. The thought of me fucking her; trying to put two and two together all the time, we only fucked with the lights out or when she decides to change in the other room, so I can't see her.

Even when we fuck in the shower, we have candles and shit everywhere, and it is always from the back. Fuck! This bitch been fucking me all this time, didn't mention one fucking thing, not that I would have fucked with her had I known but now she got Indigo knowing this shit. Anger and rage was spewing from my veins; my eyes was squinted, nose flared, seeing red like a bull in the ring. I don't think nothing can save her. "Wa...wa...wa..." Sounds like she was trying to say something, still holding on to my hands, trying to pry them off her neck. I felt like snapping her shit like a fucking chicken. Fuck does this shit make me gay? Oh

Hell no! I gotta kill her ass. How the fuck can I let her live?

"Bitch, this how you like playing with niggas huh bitch? Is this what you like to do? Why didn't you just tell me? What the fuck! Alexis why didn't you just tell me? No wonder getting fucked in the ass, was the only way you wanted to do it." Watching her continue to struggle, I just knew, if I didn't let her go right then and there. She would slip into a forever sleep. I can't have that shit on my conscience, as bad as I want to erase this bitch off the face of the earth. I just can't. Letting her go, I stumbled trying to get off top of her; watching her gasp for air and squirm around on the floor like a worm in hot ashes. Hell, I didn't know if she was going to recover, until she started coughing violently, trying to get oxygen into her lungs.

Is this motherfucker crazy? "I'm sorry" is all that she can say. What the fuck! I'm convinced she has lost her fucking marbles. Leaning backwards on the island that Jasmine and I had just previously had sex; where the remnants of her still lingered on the counter top, hearing her voice call my name, feeling her legs wrapped my damn waist and letting my tongue explore her sweet pussy. As pissed off as I am, the very thought of Jasmine has brought a calm over me like a calming sea after the storm.

"You know what I'm going to make this shit as painless for you as possible. I found out your little bullshit ass secret from Indigo so since you and her want to talk about the size of my dick. Fuck you both. I got a woman and don't want neither one of you busted up ass bitches!" The louder I screamed, the more she flinched. I knew she was a done deal, she had the look of gratitude for not killing her ass adorned all over her face. She made her way to her feet and leaned up against the wall. Still trying to catch her breath, her face was indeed busted up, big ass welts on her face, busted lip, swollen eye and busted nose. I wanted to crush her fucking brain.

"Curtis, I am truly sorry. I know you must have a lot of questions. I fucking lunged into her I was ready to choke her ass again. What the fuck I have to ask her besides the questions that I already asked her ass? I hope like hell she don't think she about to try and run a sentimental story on me like I truly give two fucks.

"Bitch! I don't want to know shit other than, why did you feel it was safe for you to keep this to yourself? You had to know this was gonna cause problems for you." "I hid it because I really wanted you and I don't identify with that part of me anymore. It's been ten years since I decided to have the operation, this is who I am Curtis. If you look closely, you can tell it is a made pussy, and not something I was born with."

"I don't give a fuck about this being who you are. You could have been you and still not even look my way. I can't believe this shit Alexis. Shit! Just gather whatever shit you got around here and get the fuck out. Please forget you ever knew me because you are already forgotten!" I was breathing hard; furious ready to take her ass down. Gritting my teeth as I spoke, all I hear is her crying and sniffing and shit. I left the room until I heard her leave the house. All I could do was pour me a shot of Hennessy. I am getting rid of

everything she used in this motherfucker. Oh! I

got a trick for that bitch Indigo as well. Let me call

her ass right now, she gonna pass out when she

hear this shit. **Ring... Ring...**

"Look Curtis don't get mad at me cause you

fucking a nigga!" This bitch got jokes I see. "Nawl,

that is not why I'm calling, but it's all good. I took

care of that shit, but check it out. Since you

spilling secrets and shit, I may as well tell you that

the only reason I started fucking with you in the

first place, was to let you know yet again, you are

fucking another man, who fucking and in love with

Jasmine." "What?" "No need to repeat all of it,

just the facts. I am in love with Jasmine Kincaid, the same person who you lost Goldie to. So sweet heart, you didn't only lose once but you lost twice. So keep your tired ass away from me, from here on out we done."

Pressing the end button and threw the phone on the bed. Coming out of my room and looked at the destruction I've caused in my house, is minor. Considering I was hell bent on taking her ass out of her misery in a body bag. Jasmine and I don't have secrets. I have known about her and her three ring circus with Indigo and Goldie from the beginning. I still for the life of me, don't understand what the fuck she see in him and still fucking me every chance she gets. That nigga

think he all that and maybe in the streets he is,

but when it comes to Jasmine, he has no idea that

she is my woman!

NO APOLOGIES

Chanta' 18

Well looks like his ass is going get a phone call, I wanted to just fuck up shit with Goldie and Jasmine. I'm still gonna tell him that she is a no nothing ass just like him, I guess that's why they are made for each other. I made the mistake of falling for a man who I knew damn well was not on the market and couldn't stay faithful if you paid him to. Then falling for Derwin I'm still falling over him everything about him exudes sex appeal from the way he dresses, the cars he drives and lawd the way he fucks me. I would have loved to met him under better circumstances cause watching the man you love go coo-coo over another woman has ran its course with me.

Loving men that is not mines has always been an issue for me. Being alone can have a person seeking out unattainable people, I am just ready to move on from this shit. My original plan was to confront him, have sex with him and let Jasmine know. Hell she know he a cheating ass nigga so that really wouldn't be a surprise to her. The next best thing would be to let him know that Jasmine is the one who is cheating and has been for years. Now that shit would crush his ass; how they deal with if after the news is out, it's their business. I would be long gone from this bullshit ass city I have had enough of the niggas and the bitches.

Sitting on my living room floor trying to figure out

how to tell Goldie about Jasmine. I wanted to go

over there but I don't want to risk her being there.

The best thing for me is to call his ass and hope he

answers or don't send my ass to voice mail.

Ring...

Ring...

"What up."

"Hey Goldie, it's Chanta'."

Damn I can't believe I am somewhat nervous.

"Okay."

NO APOLOGIES

"Well since you wanna act all nonchalant about me calling, fuck it. Jasmine skank ass is fucking this nigga named Curtis Walker and has been for years off and on. So if you really think you are her man you better second guess that shit."

Blurting that shit out I was very satisfied. I didn't give a shit how he felt now. He always trying to act like don't shit phase his ass but I bet this shit will phase his ass, knowing that his precious little Jasmine a hoe like his self. Whatever the outcome is, I'm done with all of them as well as Derwin ass, well at least until Derwin ass is over Jasmine.

NO APOLOGIES

Derwin 19

I can't believe I broke down and told Jasmine I was stalking her house for about two weeks. Every time I saw that she was seemingly getting panicked with her playing mommy. I didn't want to scare her to damn bad. My thoughts of walking up to her door, forcing my way in and taking my pussy back just didn't have the same affect on me like it did in the beginning of this operation. Chanta' has let me know that she was done with the game playing. She didn't want to have anything else to do with it unless I was done with dreaming of Jasmine.

NO APOLOGIES

I was shocked when I got a call from Jasmine, I didn't know what the hell to think when I got her phone call. Until I called her phone, I haven't heard from her since I left her house that miserable ass night that she let me go. When Jasmine called, she asked me to meet her at home which for the life of me I cannot understand why but here I am standing on the outside of her door. I'm not worried about her man cause if she thought it was going to be an issue, I wouldn't be here.

  Fuck I see her walking to the door after I have rang the doorbell. Lawd help me, I hope this is not no fuckery type shit she trying to pull.

NO APOLOGIES

"Finally you made it, took you long enough."

Was her only response when she opened the door with a royal blue lace mini dress on, with what appears to be a royal blue thong. Her nipples are hard as rocks, she is looking fucking mesmerizing. What the fuck did I just get myself into? I see she either playing with my emotions or she about to play with my dick.

"Other than you looking fucking amazing standing here in see through clothes and what not. Jasmine what the fuck is this about?"

Jasmine stood to the side to let me in. I couldn't believe I was in her home, a fucking beautiful home from what I see. Hardwood floors as far as my eyes can see, glass table top tables in the living room, pictures of them and a baby decorate the walls and plush furniture. All I could do is shake my head approving of her new way of living. She has definitely up graded but she damn sho wasn't doing bad before.

"Look Derwin I know I hurt you and I haven't stopped thinking of you and what I did. Every since you left my house that night and I know how much you really wanted to be with me and build a life with me, but I was in a situation that love had prevailed."

Jasmine spoke as she walked me down a hall that had black art on the walls into her bedroom. I was skeptical but watching her walk in front of me with all that ass saying hello to me was inviting, how the hell could I resist the ass of Jasmine Kincaid.

"Well welcome to my room and this is where I want to apologize for treating you like I did. I hope you enjoy me as much as I know I'm going to enjoy you."

After softly speaking those words she kissed me on the lips, paying special attention to top and bottom lip flicking her tongue on my lips. she dimmed the lights and turned to light the large scented candle on the nightstand. She walked behind me rubbing her hand across my chest as she kissed my neck before speaking again.

"Baby I'm going to take care of you like never before. I want you to know that I have never stopped thinking about you and I wish we could be together but because I am with Goldie we can't, but I would love to please you whenever you want me to."

What the fuck did she just say? What the fuck is going on here? Damn she just made me the happiest man in the fucking world. I wasn't expecting her to say any of this. I damn sho won't be turning anything that she wants to give me down. Hell no, I may have to share her but I be damn if I can help it to be without her. I am ready for her more than she could ever know.

"You like that baby, damn you smell good Derwin. Baby…please start unbuttoning your pants my mouth is watering just thinking about sucking your dick from the back."

Before she could finish her last word, I was dropping pants and draws to the floor. My dick bounced up and down in excitement, the mere thought of her sucking my shit from the back is about to have ready to explode. Oh shit I feel her lowering her body down, sliding her hands down the sides of my legs. Trailing her tongue down the crack of my ass nice and slow, pushing her tongue further and further, until I feel her tongue on my asshole flicking her tongue. Her hands creep up the back of my legs up to my ass seductively, separating my ass cheeks. That shit was making me sweat, every time she did that I clenched my ass cheeks together. I can't believe she doing this shit to me.

I feel her lower her head as I separate my legs she gently rubs her tongue across my balls and take each of them one by one into her mouth. She reached her hand up to my dick and pulled my dick in her direction, looking down seeing my dick disappear between my legs I must have been in heaven. Slowly she began to suck on the head teasing the head, flicking her tongue across the head. I grabbed her head to help balance her when she started deep throating me. Every time the head of my dick touched her tonsils I leaned my head back in pleasure. She was gagging, slurping on my dick making my damn toes curl, this fucking girl got skills like a porn star.

Shit she start adding speed, my knees begin to buckle. I grab a fist full of hair as I pushed her head down further. She gagged loudly while I shot hot cum down her throat.

"Ahhh.....Shit Jasmine!"

Not letting her head go until I felt all of my babies enter her mouth, my damn insides was burning up. This woman brought all kinds of emotions up out of my body, love, anger, relief, you name it she did it.

Jasmine released my dick from her mouth. She had a death grip on me as she kissed the back of my thighs, each ass cheek and for good measure licked my asshole one more time, before her lips were planting soft kisses all over my neck. She walked in front of me, kissed my lips so sexual and sucked each one of my lips so succulent, that it filled like a thousand watts of electricity was running through my fucking body. Now here I am almost out of breath and I'm ready to fuck, but she had other plans.

NO APOLOGIES

"Damn Jasmine baby I'm gonna need some of that pussy, damn that pussy is sweet and tight baby."

Practically holding my dick in one hand and holding her around her waist with the other. The look she had, told me she never stopped wanting me but she had to make the choice of a new future or stay where her heart was currently at.

"No baby no pussy right now, I just wanted you to know that I'm still here for you and I haven't left. I just had to make things seem the way he thought they would turn out. I just want you to know that we're going to have more of this.

NO APOLOGIES

Tonight was just a teaser to let you know we are unofficially-n official."

Walking back to the door, I felt like I was floating instead of walking. She let me out, walking onto the porch, I don't give a fuck I feel like a pimp right now. I just got head from the woman I love in the same fucking house she shares with her man. Shit don't get no better than that.

NO APOLOGIES

Jasmine 20

This niggas got me all fucked up. The last time I saw Derwin was a week ago. Goldie ass been MIA for a couple weeks off and on. Poor little Curtis think somehow we're going to have a relationship with his ass and especially not after I heard his ass been fucking a woman who was born a man. Shit if they ass ain't crazy, I don't know who is. Goldie is my fucking my heart but at this stage of our lives that's all he will ever be. I can't say for sure if he not fucking someone right this minute but I know him and I know how he moves and to pass up on some pussy new, old, or otherwise just ain't how he roll.

NO APOLOGIES

That is one man I will probably love for the rest of my fucking life, but I be damn if I be the fool he thinks I am. See the sad part about it is, he thinks just because I stayed all this time I wouldn't leave or couldn't leave. That's true to some extinct but why leave when I've been fucking Curtis big dick ass for years and I know Curtis loves me. He was doing him cause I was with Goldie and I understand that and I do have feelings for him. Curtis was there through all tears of my Goldie stories, he told me to leave him so many times but I didn't listen. The very first time Curtis came down to NYC, I knew we was fucking and fucking is what we did the entire weekend. From that moment on we saw each other, every other weekend while I was in college. Then it tapered off for a while but then back up again. I was not giving up the life I had created with Curtis for a lying ass Goldie who only wanted me when he was ready to fuck with me.

My aunt Fatty taught me a lot and laying down and letting a man walk over you is something you most definitely don't do, unless you got a plan B and C. I always had a plan B so all the times when Goldie was out fucking off, I always had Curtis to go to and that's exactly what I did. Some folks would say I was only using Curtis. Not at all, I was fucking a man who wanted to fuck me just as much and on many occasions he has fucked my tears away.

Derwin loved me from the very beginning, he wanted me for a while but of course I was with a man who my heart belonged to. I caught feelings for Derwin during our little stint but damn it, I would have loved to been his woman. After I let him go and then he went along fucking Chanta' ass, I knew we couldn't be in a relationship. That don't mean I won't stop fucking him...yeah he gonna get strung along too.

From the beginning I have always looked out for myself. These niggas will do as much as you let them and some gonna do the shit anyway. But to

NO APOLOGIES

each it's own. I was taught a long time ago to

depend on self and do as the fuck I please. When I

see a motherfucker ain't giving you no act right I

simply do me until I feel like I should stop, which is

rare. I don't know what the hell may happen with

any of these men in my life but what I do know is,

I will not now, not ever apologize for nothing. I

have done shit the way I want. No Apologies here!

NO APOLOGIES

One week later Jasmine & Goldie

Most of the time Goldie and I disagree on everything but in this last week we both have agreed that we were gonna stay together and do us. He brought it to my attention that he knows about me fucking Curtis and he actually heard us fucking as he left the condo Curtis live in but not before he fucked the realtor. This time around I didn't show anger, hell I wasn't even pissed I knew this day was coming. We're fucking crazy about each other and no one bitch or nigga gonna come between that. We have a relationship that only we understand and now he knows Derwin is in the picture again. He know about it but rather not hear it or see it and I couldn't agree with him more.

****

Jasmine's ass finally got my ass. It wasn't surprising when Chanta' told me about Curtis, hell I heard that nigga fuck my girl as I walked passed his place. I decided not to purchase the condo. I never want to run into Jasmine ass coming out or going in. You can't fuck over a woman for years and expect her to just be silent and do nothing.

NO APOLOGIES

Me being from the streets, I knew this shit was going to happen. I just didn't know when and how it was going to happen. I'm just glad that we were able to talk this shit out. She knows that I ain't shit, and years and years of fucking off on her, I was always ready for this shit.

If this shit don't make me straighten up and fly right, nothing will. I'm going to let her get her row out and we gonna grow together. She tried to apologize for what she did, only to be doing something I know she didn't mean. She knows she didn't mean it, now that we know all this fucked up shit about each other, there will absolutely never be NO APOLOGIES needed.

NO APOLOGIES

A note from the author

I had an amazing time writing this series, I threw some real life events in there that made a lot of people wonder about my character Jasmine... we all know a Jasmine if we weren't her ourselves.

As I write this I have just finished up two other books that are sure to drop soon the Titles are: He Thought He Had Me and Pussy Talks. Make sure you grab them they are HAWT!!!!!!!

If you can do me a big favor, once you are done reading this and any other book from me or the Black Lyfe family, please head on over to Amazon and leave a review. Those reviews help me and other Authors to know what you are looking for next and what you thought of the book you just read. It is greatly appreciated.

Also a little bit of information for the readers that are supporting me and other Authors, when you download a e-book it is imperative that you complete it till the end, or it will not and I repeat will not count for any author to get paid as a supporter you bought the e-book to support us and we greatly appreciate your efforts.

Thanks again for all of your support and be on the lookout for my next and up and coming books.

NO APOLOGIES

www.ingramcontent.com/pod-product-compliance
Lightning Source LLC
Chambersburg PA
CBHW071255250626
47159CB00004B/1187